Stranded alone in Yugoslavia, with no money, Alex Daley hadn't had any alternative to accepting the help of the overbearing Kinnan Macrae, who took her under his wing and offered her a job. But Alix had a nasty feeling it wasn't all going to be as simple as that—and how right she was!

NO ROOM IN HIS LIFE

BY

NICOLA WEST

MILLS & BOON LIMITED
15–16 BROOK'S MEWS
LONDON W1A 1DR

First published 1983
Australian copyright 1983
Philippine copyright 1983
This edition 1983

© Nicola West 1983

ISBN 0 263 74298 9

Set in Monophoto Times 10 on 10½ pt.
01–0683 – 61269

Made and printed in Great Britain by
Richard Clay (The Chaucer Press) Ltd,
Bungay, Suffolk

CHAPTER ONE

THE towering mountains, grey and barren, soared around the long, twisting bay with its islets like jewels in the sapphire waters. Boats jostled and rocked at the quayside; and Alix Daley, her long hair glinting brown and gold in the sunshine, wandered uncertainly along the broad paving, looking down into the clear water and wondering what to do next.

If only Bernie hadn't been called home, so soon after the beginning of their holiday. Maybe she ought to have gone too, Alix thought for the hundredth time. Not stayed on alone in a country where she didn't speak a word of the language, where she had no accommodation booked, no real planned itinerary. Such a holiday was fun to contemplate when there were two of them, one fluent in the German that most Yugoslavs seemed to speak. Alone, it was a different matter. But Bernie had insisted that Alix should stay on, and Alix, unwilling to oppose her friend, had agreed, albeit reluctantly. Now she was beginning to wish that she hadn't.

She sat down on a bollard, staring unseeingly at the dancing boats, her mind occupied with her problem. You can't leave now, Bernie had said. It's too beautiful to waste, one of us ought to enjoy it. And I don't know yet how serious Dad's illness is. I might be able to come back quite soon. Just keep in touch—let me know where you are—I'll probably be able to catch up with you in a couple of weeks.

Remembering that, Alix felt ashamed. After all, it wasn't *her* father who was ill; it wasn't she who had had to fly back to England after only a week of her holiday. Bernie had wanted her to stay, to enjoy the beauty and the experience of Yugoslavia—and that was what she ought to be doing now.

Determinedly, she raised her head and looked around her. It certainly was a lovely place, the Gulf of Kotor. Just about impregnable, she would have thought, with its narrow, fiord-like approach to the harbour itself, backed by almost impassable mountains. No wonder so many conquerors had been attracted to it through the ages: Turks, Venetians, Austrians, French, Russians, the British—all had reigned here, some briefly, others for long periods. Now it was Montenegrin, with only its ancient walls and buildings to testify to those bygone occupants; and, sadly, recent earthquake damage had obliterated much of its historic grandeur.

Lost in thought, Alix was not at first aware of the interested scrutiny of the man who was lying relaxed in a nearby motor-boat. Her hazel eyes were vague as she gazed around her, her heart-shaped face abstracted and thoughtful. She had dropped her blue rucksack at her feet when she sat down, and was leaning forward slightly, resting on it, her slim figure drooping a little. As he watched, she put up a slender hand to brush back the heavy fall of gold-brown hair; then glanced round and saw him.

Immediately she stiffened. This was one of the things she had dreaded without Bernie by her side. The man's stare was positively insolent! She turned away abruptly, determined not to let him throw her but feeling distinctly disturbed all the same.

Her glance had been swift but her impression of him vivid. He wasn't the sort of man you could glance at without really seeing, she thought, feeling those bright, steel-grey eyes still on her, making her skin burn with embarrassment. And that dark auburn hair, waving away from his high forehead. Unusual colouring for a Yugoslav, but she'd seen fair ones as well as dark; presumably there could be auburn too.... Not that it mattered! She shook herself impatiently. He was only a boatman—he probably hoped she'd hire him for a trip round the Bay. For a moment she was regretful; it was a lovely idea and if Bernie had been here they would undoubtedly have done so, but to hire a boat alone, with that boatman and his bright, impertinent stare. . . . With a sudden movement she came to her feet, jerking her rucksack on to her back. And although she hadn't meant to look at him again, she couldn't resist another glance at that devastatingly handsome boatman. He was still there; still watching her, with that aggravating smile playing about his wide, mobile lips. . . .

If this was going to happen all the time it would completely ruin her holiday, Alix thought angrily as she strode along the quay. In Italy, of course, it was to be expected; but she hadn't somehow thought of coming across it here in Yugoslavia. She'd expected to be treated more as an equal here—not as a sex object. That was one thing that really made her seethe!

In any case, it was time she thought of continuing her journey. She and Bernie had planned just to wander where fancy took them; working their way up the coast and into Slovenia, taking in all the contrasts of the Dalmatian coastline with its myriad islands and the clear blue waters of the Adriatic, and the high mountainous regions of the Julian Alps, close to Austria and northern Italy. They had the whole long summer holiday ahead—almost seven weeks of it. The great advantage of being a teacher, she thought gratefully. Though not the only one, of course; Alix enjoyed her job, loved the children she taught and was already collecting postcards and oddments to show the class when she returned.

Now she made her way to the bus station. Dubrovnik was her next planned stop—they had been advised to spend several days there to explore the old walled city, similar in some ways to Kotor but in a finer state of preservation—but on the way she intended to stop for a few hours in Herceg-Novi, where there were one or two interesting relics. Long journeys by local bus were tiring, she'd quickly found; it was a good idea to break them up where possible.

Before leaving, she wrote a postcard to her parents. They hadn't been keen on her coming on this long, wandering holiday, she knew, even though they knew and liked Bernie. And now that she was alone they would be doubly concerned, so she must take care to keep in touch, to let them know as often as possible that she was all right and enjoying herself. The last thing she wanted to do was to worry them; they'd had enough worry in their lives.

She thought of her parents again as she sat squashed between two silent Yugoslavs in the bus, jolting through the countryside and watching the scenery—steep cliffs on the left, falling away impossibly from the road to the white-flecked blue of the sea far below; bare, unending mountains rolling away to the right. Occasionally the road left the cliff and wandered off into the hills themselves as if following some ancient, almost invisible track. It stopped at tiny villages with houses smothered in the brilliant purples of bougainvillea and clematis. Little cottages had terraces outside, shaded by the same climbing plants, where families ate at rickety tables; fig trees grew by the roadside and old women shambled along leading donkeys laden with weeds and grasses for their feed; sometimes there was just an old woman, with no donkey but equally laden.

At least her parents had had a better life than that, Alix thought, watching with fascination as two women, almost hidden from sight in long black dresses, tugged at a reluctant mule. Though on the other hand, it was probably a matter of what you were used to; these old folk might be perfectly content with their simple lives, and never have endured the agony that could only come from the less savoury aspects of a more sophisticated life.

And it hadn't been all agony, by any means. Alix herself had had a happy childhood, warmed by the love of good parents. They had always encouraged her in whatever she wanted to do, and the sadness that had come to them all hadn't affected their own relationship. They had worked hard running the village shop, and had been respected by their friends and neighbours. They had been proud of Alix when she proved to be bright at school, delighted when she won a place at university, equally pleased when she took her Certificate of Education after gaining her degree. And although they had never suggested that she should come home at the end of her training, they had obviously been thrilled when she managed to get a job at a village primary school only ten miles away and returned to live with them.

The desperate unhappiness of that time ten years ago had left its mark on them, all the same. Alix blinked as she thought of her mother, eyes clouded with pain, watching the crocuses bloom in spring; her father, digging determinedly at that patch at the end of the garden which he would so much rather have left barren. There were still a few places they would rather not go, a few occasions they would rather forget. And it would always be the same, she reflected as the man beside her fell asleep, leaning heavily against her slim shoulder. You could never entirely recover from such a shattering experience; you would always carry it with you somewhere, however much time passed.

With an effort, she put the whole thing out of her mind. It did no good to brood. Much better to think about now—about her holiday, which she now made up her mind to enjoy, alone or not. Bernie would expect her to, after all. She must take a lot of photographs, see as much as she possibly could. She looked out of the windows with fresh determination. But the journey seemed endless; the bus was crowded, hot and stuffy; and before long Alix too found her eyelids drooping and, like the man beside her, was overcome by sleep.

She woke with a jerk to find the bus surrounded by others, the air full of fumes and noise, the people around her getting to their feet with a great deal of noise and chatter, reaching for parcels, pushing, jostling, almost forcing her to her feet and off the bus. Dazed, Alix found herself stumbling down the steps and on to a pavement. She rubbed a hand across her face and looked around, still half asleep and not sure where she was. Presumably Herceg-Novi, she thought, looking for a sign she could understand. The bus passengers had all dispersed now, leaving her alone by the dusty vehicle. As she hesitated, it began to move again and she stepped back hastily, alarmed by its nearness; and then, as it gathered speed and made for the entrance to the bus station, she remembered her rucksack, still under the seat where she had pushed it.

'Oh—no! Don't—my bag, my rucksack——' Desperately, calling uselessly, she ran after it, but there was no response from the driver and only a few curious stares from bystanders before the bus turned out on to the main road and joined the speeding traffic, to disappear from view.

Alix stood there, disbelieving and shocked. It couldn't have happened! The bus *couldn't* have just gone like that, without any warning, taking her rucksack with it. All her belongings—everything, except for the passport, camera and money she carried in her small shoulder-bag—gone, just like that. And how was she ever, without knowing a word of the language and only a little German, to make anyone understand? Where should she even begin?

Helplessly, she turned away from the road and back

to the bus station. Like most of its kind, it was a seething mass of people. Everyone was in a hurry; hurrying to look at timetables, to buy tickets, hurrying on to or off buses. Everyone seemed to know just what to do, where to go, and all the time her ears were filled with the noise of incomprehensible chatter, the roar of engines, the overriding and largely ignored announcements that came over the tannoy. Her brain spun with the sheer brutality of sound that seemed to batter at her from all sides, and she wanted nothing more than to get away, out of this suddenly hostile environment with its dust and crowds, away somewhere peaceful where she could get her bearings again.

But she couldn't do that. She had to make some effort to recover her rucksack. It contained everything she had brought for the holiday, including her travellers' cheques. Without it, she was almost destitute—and the idea of being alone and so helpless in a strange country filled her with alarm.

Surely there was someone here who could help? Surely someone could telephone ahead, to wherever the bus was going, make sure that her belongings were safe and arrange for them to be returned to her? Pulling herself together, slightly ashamed of her panic, Alix turned towards the row of booking offices. There was nothing to worry about, she scolded herself. Something could be done.

Half an hour later, exhausted by her efforts at communication and very close to tears, she wasn't so sure. It seemed that nobody at the bus station spoke English—she wasn't even sure that they knew it was English she was using. Her little knowledge of German had been worse than useless, and her phrase books apparently written in a different language from that commonly used by the Montenegrins—unless they chose deliberately not to be able to read the phrases she pointed out. In any case, none of the phrases covered her present dilemma. Pointing out the word *prtljaga*, which she was fairly sure meant luggage, and waving her hand at the bus standing empty behind her just didn't seem enough to convey to the bored clerk the enormity of what had happened.

In the end she gave up and left the building to stand looking hopelessly at the constant stream of vehicles coming and going from the big yard. Perhaps the bus she had used would come back; perhaps she might recognise the driver. Her rucksack might even be still on board. But she knew that these were faint hopes and as she stood there, too worn out even to wonder what to do next, her eyes filled with tears and she sagged against the wall.

'Excuse? You are in trouble, please?'

Startled, Alix looked round. A young sailor was standing nearby, looking at her with an anxious expression. As their eyes met he spoke again, moving a little closer.

'You are English, no? I hear you speak to the man.' He gestured towards the booking office. 'Is it something I can help?'

'Oh, how good of you,' Alix said gratefully. 'But I don't know what anyone can do. You see, I left my luggage on the bus and now it's gone and I don't know what to do. Nobody else speaks English and——' She stopped. The sailor was looking baffled; clearly his spoken English, when he had time to think it out, was better than his understanding of the language, particularly when spoken quickly and excitedly as Alix had been doing. She took a breath and started again, more slowly.

The sailor nodded. 'Yes, I understand. But the bus, it has gone, no?'

'Yes, and I don't know where,' Alix said ruefully. 'And it's got most of my money in—my rucksack, I mean. I just don't know what to do next.' And her eyes filled with tears again.

The young sailor looked worried. He glanced at his watch and said: 'I must go for my own bus soon. But perhaps you must go to the police station. They will help you there, yes?'

'Well, I suppose it's an idea,' Alix agreed slowly. 'At least they might have someone who speaks English. But I don't know where it is.'

'Oh, is easy.' He waved a hand at the main road, a busy highway which ran above the town of Herceg-Novi. 'It is just down the road, not far. You will see, it is a big new building, very modern.' He glanced again at his watch. 'And now I must go. I hope you find your baggages.'

'Thank you,' Alix said, watching him hurry away with the feeling that she had lost her only friend in the world. 'Thank you very much.'

Once again the turmoil of the bus station almost overwhelmed her. But this time there was a clear thread of positive thought in all the muddle. Now, thanks to the sailor, she had something to do—something that would at least set her back on the path to security. For with the loss of her luggage, she felt almost as if she had lost a part of herself—her identity. Get it back and she would be able to escape from this nightmare of noise and confusion and proceed with her holiday.

Following the sailor's directions, she walked out to the main road and turned left. At once she found herself facing a steady stream of fast traffic. There was no pavement; the road wasn't meant for pedestrians, and she flinched as each car or lorry thundered towards her, forcing her into a narrow belt of scrubby grass that grew under the crash barrier. But there was no other apparent way of reaching the police station, which she could already see ahead on a curve of the road. Gritting her teeth, she kept on and was thankful when, harassed and dusty, she was able to step off the road and on to the paving in front of it.

The police station was large, but seemed to be empty. Alix went in hesitantly, looking around for a reception desk. There was nothing but an empty hallway with office doors leading off it.

And now what do I do? she wondered, standing there. Knock on a door, I suppose. Her hopes of finding someone who spoke English were rapidly diminishing; she wasn't even sure of finding anyone at all. But she gathered together her courage and knocked on the first door she came to.

There was no answer. She tried another door; and another. At the third attempt, she heard the scrape of a chair inside and the door opened to reveal a swarthy Yugoslav dressed in police uniform.

'Oh, thank goodness!' Alix exclaimed, and greeted him in the only Yugoslavian words she knew. '*Dobar dan.* Do you speak English?'

The man stared at her and shook his head. I knew it, she thought, and tried again, although her German was too limited to deal with her problem. '*Sprechen sie Deutsch?*'

'*Ne.*' He shook his head and they stared at each other. The policeman was obviously at a loss. He could hardly go back into his office and leave her standing there; yet there was nothing more either of them could say. In the end, more to break the silence than anything else, she thought, he asked her a question. Alix shook her head and shrugged helplessly, and they continued to gaze at each other.

Then she heard a door somewhere in the depths of the building open and close. Voices sounded in the corridor that led off the hallway. Alix looked at the policeman with sudden hope, and they both turned to see who was coming.

As the two men came into view round the corner, Alix caught her breath and stared in astonishment. It couldn't be—it had to be his double, perhaps his

brother or a cousin. But there was no doubt that she
had seen those light grey eyes, bright as sharpened steel,
before—and that dark, waving auburn hair. And—she
felt herself colour even as she recognised it—that oddly
disturbing, assessing gaze.

The boatman from Kotor, accompanied by a
policeman who even Alix could see was of some high
rank, stood before her in the corridor of the Herceg-
Novi police station, a glint of laughter in his eyes as
they met hers. And a wave of futile anger swept over
her as she stared back. Why did it have to be *him*? And
what possible help could *he* be to her?

CHAPTER TWO

ALIX'S policeman broke into a flood of Yugoslavian. She stood by, wondering what he was saying, since he could have gleaned no information at all from her, and saw the concern on the senior policeman's face, the look of mocking amusement on that of the boatman. Just as well she *hadn't* hired his boat, she thought indignantly. That was just the kind of buccaneering type one didn't want to find oneself at sea with! She caught his glance again and her face burned at the way his glance roved casually over her. Oh, what was the use of standing here? No one was going to help her, it was plain, and all the time her rucksack was getting farther and farther away.

All three were now engaged in earnest conversation. Perhaps they'd forgotten all about her. She might as well go—find her way back to the town, where perhaps she could find a tourist office where they could speak English and would try to help her. In any case, she would have to do something soon—it was already well into the afternoon and there would soon be the problem of the night to consider. She wasn't even sure that she had enough money on her to cover a night's stay in the cheapest private room.

She turned, meaning to slip out while they were engrossed in their talk. But the boatman was quicker than she had expected. With a lithe, sinuous movement, he was at her other side, his hand on her wrist.

'Let go!' Alix cried, outraged. She twisted round to glare at the two policemen. 'Make him let go!' Even with language difficulties, they must surely understand what she was saying. 'Let go at *once*, do you understand?'

'Sure I understand.' The voice, cool, lazy and unmistakably English, came as a shock. Feeling almost as if she had been hit by a jet of ice-cold water, Alix stared at him, her wrist suddenly limp under his iron-hard fingers. 'Don't get into such a fuss, kid. It's all right. I'm not going to do anything to you here, am I!'

Alix blinked up at him, aware suddenly of his size, of the sheer masculinity that emanated from him. The grey eyes met hers, grave now but still with a glint of laughter lurking in them, and her shock was replaced by a surge of annoyance. How dared he laugh at her? Who was he anyway—and what was he? Yugoslav or English? Boatman or—what?

'Look, you might find this all very funny, but I don't!' she snapped. 'Why didn't you say you were English? Jabbering away there in Serbo-Croat or whatever it was! Didn't it strike you that I must be in some sort of trouble, or I wouldn't be here? That you could help me, since I haven't found anyone who could speak even a word of English? Or maybe that's all part of the joke to you, is that it? Well, have a good laugh, and tell your friends the joke too so that they can join in, and then maybe you could spare a moment or two to give me a bit of help. I should think I'd have earned it in entertainment value alone, wouldn't you?'

To her fury she felt the tears in her eyes again, and she turned away. But, gently but firmly, the pressure on her wrist forced her to turn back and she looked up into eyes that were entirely serious now.

'All right,' he said quietly. 'I didn't mean to upset you—but I didn't even know you were English until you spoke. How could I? It was the first time I'd heard your voice, the *policajca* didn't know, and your clothes don't exactly give you away.' Alix glanced down at her dusty jeans and loose shirt and had to admit that it was more or less uniform over the entire Continent. 'But now we know where we are, why don't you tell me your problem? As you've heard, I'm pretty fluent myself, so I can probably help as much as anyone.'

He let go of her wrist and Alix stood rubbing it thoughtfully and trying to collect her thoughts. The nearness of the man she had taken for a boatman still disturbed her; there was a magnetism about him that she had never sensed before, and she was aware of a tingling through her nerves, as if she had been stripped of a layer of skin so that they were nearer the surface than usual. And the revelation that he was English after all had turned all her assumptions upside down.

The three men were all watching her. She glanced around at them and bit her lip.

'I—I've lost my luggage,' she blurted out at last. 'On the bus from Kotor. I fell asleep—I was still dozey when we arrived and everyone got off—I didn't really realise what was happening, and then the bus went and I realised my rucksack was still on board. I tried to stop it, but the driver didn't understand and I couldn't find anyone who spoke English.'

'I see.' He nodded quickly and turned to the two policemen, breaking into a flood of Serbo-Croat. All three then began to talk at once, with a great deal of gesticulation on the part of the two policemen. Unable to understand a word, Alix could nevertheless gain a lot of information from their expressions. From their outspread hands, their shrugs and pursed mouths, she knew their verdict before the Englishman turned back to her.

'They don't see a lot of hope,' he told her. 'The bus probably went on to Dubrovnik and may have picked up passengers on the way. The best bet is to go on to Dubrovnik and enquire there. It may have been handed in. But I'm afraid it's quite likely to have been just quietly removed by some sharp-eyed passenger. Was there much in it?'

'Only my entire wardrobe,' Alix said ruefully. 'Plus

my travellers' cheques.' She bit her lip again. 'Do you think it will have been handed in at Dubrovnik?'

'There's always a chance. Yugoslavians are pretty honest generally. But there's always the odd one—and there are plenty of foreigners about too. And without knowing the language it's difficult to trace anything getting lost.'

'You can say that again,' Alix said with feeling. 'Well, I suppose that's what I'd better do, then—go on to Dubrovnik and try there. I just hope I've enough money in my bag.'

The copper-haired man looked down at her, his expression concerned. 'You mean that without your rucksack you're more or less destitute? You've no more money?' His expression changed as Alix nodded. 'God, you kids! Don't you ever think ahead? You come swanning over on to the Continent, unable to speak a word of anything useful, and then when something goes wrong you're helpless. And it's suckers like me that have to turn to and look after you, just as if we don't have enough problems of our own!' He sighed. 'All right, come on. I'll see you get to Dubrovnik, and I'll see that you don't have to sleep on the beach. I'll even help you try to trace this rucksack of yours.' He turned to the policemen and spoke a few crisp words before taking her arm and turning her towards the door. 'You'd better tell me your name, and I warn you I'm in a hurry now. Not all of us are here on holiday!'

'Now look!' They were out of the police station before Alix, rendered momentarily speechless with fury at his high-handed attitude, was able to speak at all. 'I don't know who you think you are, but you don't have to talk to me like that! And neither do I have to come with you. Just what do you think you're doing, taking me over like this? Okay, you helped me back there—but that doesn't mean you're in charge of me! I can look after myself.'

'And that I doubt,' he retorted, stopping in front of a sleek red Audi and unlocking the passenger door. 'And don't imagine I *want* to take you over, as you put it. There's nothing I want less than a job as a nanny, believe me. But if I hadn't, those two coppers would have asked me to, just because I'm a fellow-countryman of yours and because they wanted you off their backs—and who can blame them for *that*? And knowing the kind of hassle you could get yourself into, left to your own devices—well, I wouldn't leave a kitten to wander round a motorway on its own, would I?'

He pushed Alix into the car and slammed the door on her. Alix immediately began to fiddle with the lock, but before she could open it he was in the driver's seat beside her, reaching across to fasten her safety-belt. Once again his nearness set up that disturbing prickle under her skin; she felt his fingers brush lightly across her body and shivered.

'I told you, I can look after myself,' she began coldly, but he interrupted it with a snort and a shrug.

'Then that's something we'll never get to find out, isn't it? Because I don't intend to leave you wandering around Herceg-Novi on your own, and that's final.' His glance as he turned to her was scathing. 'Have you any idea what you look like? An urchin, that's what! Nobody would take you seriously for a minute—and do you really think anyone would take you in and give you a room, looking like that? The Yugoslavs have a healthy respect for convention, or haven't you been here long enough to realise that yet? Anything out of line and they get very suspicious. Or maybe you fancy sleeping rough and getting woken up by a *policaja* in the small hours? Use your head, little girl, and do as you're told for once!'

Alix drew a deep breath, but before she could let fly he had started the engine and gunned the car out of the forecourt. The silence seethed between them as they swept down the fast road and curved towards the shining blue of the sea, and for a moment Alix's fury was overcome by the beauty of the scene before her. But before they had gone another mile, she had found her voice.

'Where are we going?'

'Dubrovnik, of course,' he answered tersely. 'And you needn't sound so suspicious—I'm not going to whisk you into the mountains and have my wicked way with you. Though I might be tempted to dunk you in some mountain stream and give you a good wash.' He checked suddenly and glanced at her, a twitch of amusement pulling at his lips. 'I've just had a thought! I suppose you were telling the truth? You really are alone? There's not some pal of yours waiting back in Herceg-Novi to see if you've been successful in pulling some confidence trick, is there?'

'There certainly is not!' Indignation jerked the truth from Alix's lips before it occurred to her that a lie at that point might have got her free of this overbearing, impossible man. 'I did have a friend with me—but Bernie had to fly back to England. So we decided I should carry on on my own.'

'Very unselfish of Bernie,' he drawled, and something in his tone puzzled Alix. 'And what were you doing, just wandering?'

'Yes,' she answered defensively. 'Neither of us likes organised holidays. And there are plenty of places in Yugoslavia doing bed and breakfast—well, bed, anyway. It's easy enough to find accommodation.'

'Oh, sure,' he agreed, keeping his eyes straight ahead. 'Though not quite so easy to find single rooms, I imagine.'

'Well, that didn't matter, we always share,' Alix answered, still puzzled by his manner. Then she glanced at him and caught his expression, and light hit her. Of course! He thought Bernie was a *boy-friend*! A chuckle almost escaped her as she thought of Bernie—short for Bernice—slim, willowy and most definitely female, with a mop of ash-blonde hair and huge blue eyes that were capable of turning heads a mile away. Not that that ever bothered Bernie. She was as cool as they came, and well able to look after herself; better than me, Alix thought wryly. Bernie would never have left her rucksack on a bus, would never have got into such a state about it if she had and, offered a lift by a devastatingly handsome man in an Audi, would have captivated him in moments. And would certainly never, never have been called an urchin, however dishevelled she might have become.

His expression was still carefully noncommittal and Alix was on the point of telling him the truth when she stopped herself. Let him think what he liked—what did it matter anyway? It might even be a good thing if he did think she had a boy-friend, liable to return and reclaim her at any time. Not that she intended to see any more of him once they had reached Dubrovnik. There were bound to be people there who could help her, and even if she couldn't trace her rucksack there must be some way of getting enough money to continue with her holiday.

'Look, we'd better introduce ourselves,' he said abruptly. 'I'm Kinnan Macrae. What's your name?'

'Alix. Alix Daley,' she said reluctantly, not wanting to give him even this small part of herself. Wasn't there some tribe who never spoke their real names because they believed it gave an enemy power over them? She knew how they felt; and power was the last thing she wanted this—this Kinnan Macrae to have over *her*. 'I'm a teacher,' she added hurriedly, to show him that she wasn't a helpless child. But his reaction seemed to indicate that even this had failed.

'Good God! I must be older than I thought. Or is it just policemen that look younger as you age? Have you actually taught yet, or have you just finished training?'

'I've been teaching for a year,' she said coldly. 'I'm twenty-three, if you must know, and I have an English degree.'

'My, my,' he mocked infuriatingly. 'A real little bluestocking! And I took you for no more than sweet seventeen. But now that you mention it, I can see those little tell-tale wrinkles! And the frown lines come, no doubt, from too much poring over books by the light of one dim lamp.'

'Any frown lines you see come from having to listen to you talking drivel!' she snapped. 'Look, I don't know what it is you've got against me, Mr Maclean——'

'Macrae. Kinnan Macrae. Call me Kinnan if you find it easier.'

'I don't!' Aggravated almost beyond control, she sought for words. She had forgotten what she was going to say and nothing coherent came to her mind now, so that she had to subside, knowing that Kinnan Macrae was laughing at her. Why on earth had she agreed to come with him? Come to that, she *hadn't* agreed—she'd been forced. More or less kidnapped—and under the eyes of two policemen, too! Well, he wouldn't catch her next time. She'd be out of this car at the first opportunity, make no mistake about that, and it would take a whole police force plus a herd of wild horses to get her back in again.

The road had left the coast now and wandered off into the hills, twisting along the contours. To their right fields stretched away into the distance, the horizon bordered by a vast range of grey mountains. Alix stared at them, awed by the immensity they represented; an immensity not just of sheer size, but of distance and area too. How far did the wilderness extend, she wondered, and what must it be like to live in such a place?

Kinnan Macrae caught her glance and seemed to understand what was going through her mind.

'Tremendous, isn't it?' he remarked. 'Makes you wonder how anyone ever thought they could conquer the whole place. There must always have been pockets of resistance to the invader. Look at the last war—even with the technology they had then, the Germans could never subdue Yugoslavia. And the wild grandeur, the sheer implacability of the country seeps into its people too. They respond to leadership, never to bullying; even the poorest of them is too proud for that.'

'It's a wonderful country,' Alix said softly. 'I've only been here for a few days—but I loved it from the first.'

He glanced at her. 'What were you planning to do? Just wander?'

'Yes, but we did have some loose plans. We wanted to make our way more or less up the coast and then strike up into Slovenia. Do some walking in the Bled—Bohinj area. I've heard that's very beautiful.'

'It is. Rather Austrian—as indeed it was, once. And do you plan to carry on alone?'

Alix shrugged. 'That was the idea. I wasn't too sure, but Bernie insisted, said it was a waste for both of us to go back. Anyway, Mr Allan—Bernie's father—might recover and then Bernie would be able to come back.' She hid a smile, thinking how neatly she had avoided mentioning Bernie's sex. It was amusing her now to play Kinnan Macrae along. And it didn't matter—once they reached Dubrovnik she would be parting from him, never to see him again. She ignored the slight inexplicable pang this thought gave her. She didn't like Kinnan Macrae, that was for sure, but his company was stimulating to say the least. And she had to admit that, arrogant and aggravating as he was, he was certainly being helpful. If only he could help her trace her rucksack—then she would be able to say goodbye and go on her way, free of him.

Neither spoke for a while. Alix, busy with her own thoughts, gazed out of the window, registering the wildness of the scenery, the fields of vines and olive groves that surrounded each small community. Kinnan was evidently occupied with thoughts of his own as he drove, keeping his eyes firmly on the road. What thoughts they might be, Alix had no idea. She wondered what he was doing here, how it had come about that he should be relaxing in a boat at Kotor, only to turn up at Herceg-Novi police station a few hours later. He could be no ordinary holidaymaker, surely; he seemed to know the place too well, and the language too. All very mysterious—but a glance at his stern profile told her that he didn't intend mentioning his affairs to her, and she dared not ask.

The last part of the journey took them back to the sea-cliffs once more. Alix watched spellbound as they twisted along the narrow road, far above the dark blue sea. Hundreds of feet below, she could see the creamy lace of the waves as they broke against rocks or the occasional golden strand. Small fishing villages huddled at the water's edge, one or two of them boasting modern hotels that indicated their part in the tourist trade. And then the road twisted again and they came within sight of Dubrovnik itself, and Alix gasped with delight.

The sun was lower in the sky now, casting the rich orange glow of evening over the whole scene. A pathway of topaz burned its way across the waters, setting fire to each rippling wave. The western horizon was already aflame, a tawny backcloth to a stage set for a hundred operettas. And in the foreground, standing out from the shore as proudly as a great ship under full sail, lay the old city of Dubrovnik, its walls silhouetted against the fiery sky, its towers bastions of strength and stubborn determination protecting the tiny harbour. It looked almost unreal, a picture from some artist's romantic imagination. Alix imagined those ancient walls patrolled by guards, that harbour besieged by invading ships. What battles must have raged here; how the inhabitants must have fought to keep their city and their independence. Even now, the city was being invaded, a peaceful invasion this time of tourists like herself, welcomed by the inhabitants, entertained and fed. She found herself hoping fervently that it would stay that way; that all Dubrovnik's future invasions would be as peaceful.

Kinnan said nothing as he drove down the steep cliff road towards the city, and Alix watched as the ancient walls came closer, drinking in their beauty. The road passed outside them, under a soaring hill, and she caught one glimpse of a huge gateway and a bustling square before the old city was behind them and they were driving through more ordinary streets.

'Are you taking me straight to the bus station?' she asked, coming back to earth.

Kinnan shook his head. 'I think you need to freshen up a bit first. You've had a pretty strenuous day, one way and another. When did you last eat?'

Alix thought. 'At Kotor. I was going to have lunch at Herceg-Novi.' No wonder she felt lightheaded! It was already evening and she hadn't eaten since breakfast. Somehow she'd forgotten about food, but now she felt hungry. And with hunger came anxiety. Was she going to have enough money to pay for both a meal and a room for the night? And, if her rucksack wasn't returned, what then?

'Don't worry,' Kinnan said suddenly, laying a hand on her knee. 'I've had an idea. I'd like to talk to you about it before you decide anything.'

'An idea?' A strange tingle ran through her body as he touched her. 'What do you mean? Look, I'm not asking to borrow money from you, you've done enough——'

'I'm not offering to lend it.' His tone was dry as he swung the car round a corner and into view of another harbour, larger than the one at the old city, with yachts of all shapes and sizes moored along its quay and the dim shapes of cruise liners further along. Alix watched, bemused, as the Audi swept along the quayside and then stopped a few yards from a sleek white yacht that glowed in the fading evening light, its smooth, upswept lines indicating a potential power and speed combined with beauty that brought an ache to her throat.

'This is Gruz,' Kinnan told her briefly, 'Dubrovnik's main harbour. And you're looking at my ketch, *Manta*. I thought you'd welcome a wash and something to eat.'

Alix stared at the yacht. It was about fifty feet long, she judged, and in perfect condition, its white paint gleaming in the soft harbour lights. She gazed in delight at the clean lines. All her life she had loved boats and had sailed with her uncle while on holiday at his home on the Solent, though she'd never had the chance to even step aboard a boat like this. But even as she opened the car door and got out, her legs stiff from the long drive, she hesitated. How did she know this one really belonged to the man at her side? And did he have any ulterior motive in inviting her aboard? She'd already likened him to a buccaneer, a pirate, in her mind. Wouldn't it be better to go now, to thank him politely for his help and the lift, ask the way to the bus station and take it from there?

She shivered suddenly. The thought of being alone again, trying desperately to communicate in a foreign land, chilled her weary body. And then Kinnan, behind her, said brusquely:

'Well, don't stand there all night. I'm hungry, if you're not. This way.'

He led the way across the quayside to the ketch; and Alix, her doubts unresolved but put aside, followed him.

She was surprised at the neatness and the luxury of the yacht. From the deckhouse, she followed Kinnan down into a saloon, unexpectedly spacious, with a

central table and two berths, one on either side, used as
seating during the daytime. Above the berths were
cupboards and the saloon was tidy and uncluttered.
Kinnan was already lighting a lamp, and, as Alix came
through the hatch, he jerked his head.

'You can wash through there—shower if you like.
Can't offer you a change of clothing, I'm afraid, unless
you'd like to borrow a shirt. I imagine my jeans are
rather too big for you.'

'I should think so.' He was at least twice her size, so
they had to be. But a clean shirt would be a comfort.
'I'm not staying, though,' she reminded him. 'I'd better
not borrow anything.'

'Suit yourself.' He was busy in one of the cupboards
now and Alix felt suddenly hungry at the sight of eggs,
cheese and salad vegetables being brought out. She
opened the door he had indicated and found herself in a
washroom that must have been the smallest she'd ever
seen. Every inch of its limited space had been used, and
there was everything anyone could wish for. The shower
was efficient and soothing; she stood under it for as
long as she dared until she suddenly wondered where
the water came from and in the cause of economy
hastily turned it off. It was rather a let-down to have to
get back into her grubby clothes; she made a face as she
climbed into dusty jeans and shirt again. But at least
she was clean underneath, and the knowledge gave her
the confidence she needed to face Kinnan again.

He was just putting a meal on the saloon table when
she emerged—omelettes and salad, with cheese, fruit
and a bottle of wine. Just what she needed, Alix
thought, tucking in. But she mustn't stay here too long.
There was still the problem of accommodation for
tonight.

'How far is the bus station?' she asked, finishing the
apple she had chosen for dessert. 'I'm getting worried
about my things. Even if they've been handed in, it

might be too late to get them tonight, and I have to find somewhere to stay too.'

'You don't need to worry about that,' he told her casually. 'You can stay here.'

'Here? On your boat?' The suggestion was so fantastic that she laughed.

'What's the joke? It's a perfectly reasonable idea. Even if you get your rucksack back, you might find it difficult to find a room at this time of day. And if you don't. . . .' He shrugged. 'I don't really know what you're going to do, do you? And it's a perfectly genuine offer.'

'Yes, I realise that,' said Alix after a pause. 'I'm sorry, but I really couldn't. You've done enough——'

'Fiddlesticks!' His tone was rough and she subsided. For a moment there was silence; then he glanced at her under heavy brows and said abruptly: 'Look, I told you I had an idea. I was going to leave it until we saw whether your rucksack turned up—but I've an idea that if it does you're going to just take off into the blue on your own, and that wouldn't be a good thing. So let's discuss it now, before we go any further.'

'Discuss what?' Alix demanded. Feeling better after her wash and meal, she was ready to argue again. 'I don't see that there's anything to discuss.'

'That's because you haven't listened to me yet,' he said calmly. 'That's the way to find things out, you know, as I'm sure you're always telling your pupils. What age are they, by the way?'

'Five. The reception class,' Alix said tersely. 'Look, Mr Macrae——'

'I thought you agreed to call me Kinnan.'

'I did no such thing. And if you'll stop interrupting, we can clear this up once and for all. I'm very grateful to you for bringing me to Dubrovnik and for giving me this meal and letting me wash here. But I really can't ask you to do any more. If you'll just tell me the way to the bus station——'

'And if *you'll* just listen to *me*,' he broke in, 'you'll find that most of what you're saying is quite unnecessary. Yes, of course I'll take you to the bus station, of course I'll help you over your luggage. But before then I want to put something to you. And I think you'll find it's an offer you can't refuse.'

Alix stared at him and the blood came into her cheeks. Offer? What kind of offer could he mean? She could think of only one kind herself, and her face burned as she scrambled to her feet, narrowly missing bumping her head on the swinging lamp, and turned towards the companionway.

'It seems you've made a mistake about me, Mr Macrae,' she said coldly. 'I'm not interested in any offers of the kind you're about to make. In any case, I've already told you, Bernie's quite likely to come back again soon.' Thank goodness she'd allowed him to go on believing in Bernie as her boy-friend, she thought breathlessly—and then gave a tiny scream as he moved to reach the gangway before her, his hands closing over her wrists.

'Let *go*!' she panted, twisting away from him in the narrow space. 'You're hurting me!'

'Then stop panicking and listen.' His voice was maddeningly cool. 'You jump to too many conclusions, little Miss Muffet. I'm not asking you to provide me with a night's entertainment in return for my kindness—I don't have to be that hard up. I'm making a serious business proposition.'

'A business——?'

'That's what I said.' He forced her back into her seat. 'Look, I'm in a bit of a spot myself. Maybe it never struck you to wonder why I was in that police station. You haven't been the only one to run into trouble, you know!'

Alix stared at him. 'I did wonder,' she admitted. 'But in any case, I don't see——'

'I told you, listen.' His voice was curt and anger seethed in her again. Just who did he think he was, talking to her like that? But her annoyance was forgotten as he spoke. 'First of all, I'm not here on holiday. I've got a job of work to do. I'm a TV journalist and naturalist, and I'm making a film on underwater life—marine biology. I've been here a couple of weeks, sussing out the area, seeing where would be best for what I want to portray—that's why I was in Kotor when you first saw me.' His eyes glinted as Alix blushed again. 'Oh yes, I remember you there— and you remembered me, didn't you, for all your haughty ice-maiden act! Anyway, we've been getting along fine, but a couple of days ago we struck trouble. My two assistants were driving down to Kotor to meet me there, and they had a road accident. Not too serious, thank God, but bad enough to set them on a plane back to England—a couple of broken bones, that sort of thing. Well, I'm having some others flown out, but meanwhile I'm stuck. Can't get on with the work satisfactorily alone—and that's where you come in.'

'Me? But I'd be no good——'

'I can be the best judge of that. I don't want you to do anything technical—I'll have to wait for that. But you could help me on some of the preliminary work— and by seeing to things here for me, the cooking and so on, so that I can be getting on with the writing. I'll be narrating my own script, and it's a complex business.' He paused for a moment and then added: 'I realise this is meant to be your holiday. But I think I can promise you an interesting few days—I'll be taking a trip or two to the islands, and there'll be plenty of swimming and sunbathing. And you can have time to explore Dubrovnik itself, of course.'

'Yes . . . we did mean to spend a few days here,' Alix murmured. She felt dazed by Kinnan Macrae's suggestion, unable to know just what to make of it. On the face of it, it seemed genuine enough . . . so why did she have this uncomfortable feeling that there was something else behind it? Some stronger reason that he hadn't mentioned? And why, when mind and reason argued so strongly in favour of accepting the offer, did every instinct in her body cry out to her against it?

Kinnan had let go of her wrists and she sat there, looking at him, trying to discover what lay behind those enigmatic eyes. It was all so simple as he expressed it. A few days' accommodation, a job which seemed as if it would scarcely impinge at all on her holiday . . . time to sort out her own affairs, get some more money to replace what she'd lost, make up her mind what to do next. Even time, perhaps, for Bernie to return, ready to start their holiday afresh.

Could it possibly be that simple? Or would she be wiser to say no, to continue trying to trace her luggage, find a room somewhere for the night and get help tomorrow from a local tourist office or even the British Consulate, if there was one here?

But she knew already that she couldn't face coping with all that alone. Not tonight, anyway. There was no certainty that the bus station would be able to help her at this hour, even if her rucksack had been found, and common sense told her that finding a room without luggage would be difficult. Especially as she was not at all sure that she had enough money to pay for it. It seemed that she had little option but to accept Kinnan Macrae's offer—for tonight, at any rate.

I ought never to have stayed on alone, she thought miserably. I just can't cope on my own. Bernie would have known just what to do.

Kinnan was watching her, saying nothing, waiting for her to speak. At last he said, his voice oddly gentle: 'That's settled, then, is it? And I'll go to the bus station with you tomorrow—or straightaway if you prefer, though I'm not sure we'd get very far at this time of night.'

Don't do it, a small voice inside her urged. Don't say yes. But a wave of exhaustion swept over her even as she opened her mouth to refuse, and she felt her eyelids droop.

Kinnan nodded, as if satisfied. Then to her infinite horror, he came round the saloon and scooped her into his arms as if she were a child. And although she wanted to protest—knew that she must protest—Alix found her head dropping against his chest as if she had come home; and felt, rather than saw, as he carried her through a door into another cabin and laid her gently on the bunk there.

The sun was bright at the windows when she woke, and she was conscious of an odd rocking motion that was difficult to place at first. She opened her eyes and stared in bewilderment round the small cabin, taking in the white bulkhead, the fixed wardrobe and chest of drawers in glowing teak, the air of subtle luxury that she had noticed last night in other parts of the ketch. Then memory flooded back, and she sat bolt upright, rigid with dismay.

She had spent the night here! On Kinnan Macrae's yacht! And he—he must have put her to bed himself, for she had no recollection of getting here by herself. Her heart beating wildly, she let the sheet fall and looked down at herself. She was wearing her flimsy pants and bra—mere scraps of lace. *He* must have removed her jeans and shirt, lifted her into this bunk— and what else mightn't he have done while she was so sleepy? Slender hands covered her burning face. Well, there was one thing certain. She couldn't stay *here* any longer!

She lay back, recalling her feelings of the evening before. She'd been exhausted, suddenly worn out by all that had happened. The journey to Yugoslavia, the few days before Bernie had been called home; her indecision about whether to stay; her doubts about the wisdom of continuing alone. And then yesterday, losing her luggage and meeting the most disturbing man she had ever encountered—all had taken its toll. She even remembered feeling helpless, unable to cope. Well, all that would be changed now. She was back to her normal self, capable and efficient. Briskly she got out of bed and pulled on her jeans.

It was several moments later that she discovered the loss of her passport.

Throughout all the trauma of losing most of her possessions yesterday, Alix had been sustained and comforted by the fact that her passport had been in the shoulder-bag she carried. As long as she had that, she felt, things couldn't be too desperate. Now it had gone—and it didn't take too many guesses to say where. There was only one man who could have taken it—the man who had brought her here, half against her will, yesterday, who had made that fantastic suggestion that she should stay, spun her that story about being a naturalist and photographer. Kinnan Macrae.

Alix felt her whole body chill to ice. Just what and who *was* Kinnan Macrae, really? And why was he so set on keeping her with him?

CHAPTER THREE

RAPIDLY, Alix finished dressing and washed in the tiny basin. Her heart was thumping with anger and apprehension as she opened the door and marched out into the saloon. This time she would get things absolutely clear with the overbearing Kinnan Macrae! He would find that she wasn't the scared, bewildered little *urchin* he'd thought her. Alix Daley was all woman—all *liberated* woman, she told herself fiercely, no man's toy and well able to look after herself.

She was somewhat deflated to find the saloon empty, the table laid neatly with a checked cloth, a jug of orange juice, some fresh rolls and a pot of cherry jam. The scent of coffee drifted in from the tiny galley, but there was no sound, and Kinnan was clearly not below decks.

Alix glanced at the breakfast he had left for her. It was tempting—but she couldn't sit here and eat while doubts tormented her. She had to know why he had taken her passport—and then she had to get away. Because every instinct in her body was screaming at her that Kinnan Macrae was dangerous—and that if she didn't get away soon, she never would. . . .

She ran up the steps and out on deck, then stopped, catching her breath. The harbour was alive with sunlight, searing through the cerulean sky, dancing on a million tiny wavelets as they rippled from boat to boat. On the far side, trees fringed the horizon with dark green; beyond them the mountains swept away into the distance. The yachts that lined the quayside were alive with people, swabbing decks, doing the chores, calling cheerfully to each other, or merely sunbathing. And on the shore was a market, gay with scarlet umbrellas and piles of colourful fruit and vegetables, loud with laughing abuse in which Yugoslavs everywhere seemed to delight.

'Looking for someone?'

The cool voice jerked her back to her own problems and she whipped round to find Kinnan lounging on the coachroof, his back against the deckhouse, a notepad on his knee. He was looking up at her coolly, yet still with that glint of laughter in his eyes that annoyed her so. She glowered down at him, noticing even at this moment how infuriatingly handsome he was, with his dark chestnut hair waving smoothly back from his high forehead, his heavy brows lifted to reveal ice-grey eyes. He was wearing faded denim shorts that showed his muscular thighs, and the upper part of his body, equally well muscled and coated with golden hairs, was naked. No man had the right to look like that, she thought, turning away abruptly. It was too distracting.

'Had your breakfast?' Kinnan enquired lazily. 'Marvellous morning, isn't it?'

'No—yes,' she answered in confusion. 'I mean no, I haven't had breakfast, and yes, it's a lovely morning.' She recalled why she had come on deck and turned to face him. 'Mr Macrae, what have you done with my passport?'

Kinnan closed his eyes. 'Please, I really would prefer you to call me Kinnan. I fully intend to call you Alix, so you might as well—and it's so much friendlier on a small boat.'

'There's no need to worry about that,' Alix gritted between her teeth, 'because I don't intend to stay on your boat for one moment longer than I can help. Just as soon as you've given my passport back, I'll be off. You won't need to bother with me any longer, and——'

'Oh?' he said, his eyebrows raised with a quirk that

made his face even more attractive. 'But I offered you a job.'

'Which I haven't accepted!' she snapped.

'But I thought you had.' With a lithe movement, he was on his feet, towering over her, one hand gripping the rail at each side of her so that she was trapped. 'I was quite sure you had,' he repeated softly.

Alix stared up at him. Her heart was hammering painfully, her breath coming with a rapidity that scared her. His nearness set up a tingling over her whole body. She looked into his eyes, past the dark fringe of lashes to the cool grey; but the expression in them, amused and faintly enigmatic, made her drop her glance and she found herself gazing instead at the powerful column of his neck, the pulsing Adam's apple, and the gleaming, tanned skin of his broad chest.

He moved a little closer, so that his arms brushed against hers, warm from the morning sunlight, and the points of her breasts touched his skin. The yacht seemed to shift suddenly and she turned her head wildly from side to side as if to escape. She thought briefly of calling for help, but there was no one within earshot, and in any case who would take any notice of her among all the other sounds of the harbour? Almost without realising it, she was leaning back over the rail; she felt Kinnan's body closer against hers and realised with a kind of despair that she could move no farther away from him. Imploringly, she looked up at his face, her hazel eyes wide in her small face, and saw that he was bending his head towards her almost as if against his own will. Her lips parted in protest and were silenced as his own claimed them, softly at first and then with increasing passion; and Alix felt herself swept up in a whirl of conflicting emotion. As his hands left the rail so that his arms could fold around her, there was nothing she could do but cling to him. Her body moulded to his, contours meeting in curves that had an entirely unexpected sweetness, and as he moved against her a shaft of pure delight coursed through her body, stilling all her qualms, quelling all reason so that all her doubts and apprehensions were overwhelmed by this new sensuality. Her fingers tangled in his thick waving hair as she let her lips part willingly under his, and she felt the groan that tore through them without knowing if it came from his throat or her own.

With one hand, Kinnan traced a pathway of fire down her side, skimming her breast and sleeking the line of her thigh. He drew her closer still and his lips left hers to plant a trail of kisses down the length of her slim neck and into the collar of her shirt. With his teeth, he nipped open the buttons to explore further, and Alix hung across his arm as his free hand came up to pull the fabric away from her breast. Then, as he lifted his head to gaze once more into her eyes, she heard a call from a nearby yacht; and although she knew that they were sheltered from view, the colour flooded her cheeks and she stiffened in his arms.

'Kinnan,' she whispered agonisedly. 'Not here—stop, please——' She scarcely knew what she was saying; her own response had dazed her and she was conscious only of his nearness, of her thudding heart and a strong surge of desire unlike anything she had ever before experienced. But as she looked into his eyes, sanity began to reassert itself and she felt her body stiffen. What was she doing—what were they both doing? Oh, maybe she shouldn't be surprised at him—wasn't this what she'd suspected he was after all along? But herself—what had got into her, to allow him to behave like this, to behave like it herself? Colour flooded into her face and she turned away from his scrutiny, aware that she had given him every help in putting her at a disadvantage.

'Where do you suggest, then?' he murmured. 'Below decks? Sounds a good idea to me.' And he drew away from her, still keeping a firm grip around her waist, and made to lead her down the steps.

'*No!*' Feverishly she pulled away from him. 'I didn't mean that—I meant—oh, stop looking at me like that—look, please give me my passport and let me go—*please!*'

'Let you go?' he mocked. 'But it was just getting interesting.'

'And don't *laugh* at me!' she stormed. 'I just want to get away, can't you understand that? Away from your boat and you—as far away as possible. I don't know who you are——'

'But I told you.'

'And I don't believe you!' Her hazel eyes darkened as she stared at him and let all her misgivings come to the surface. 'All right, you may be who you say you are, you may even be making a film of sorts—but you're not really working for a living, Kinnan Macrae. You're just a rich, idle playboy, whiling away the time instead of getting on with a proper job. You're——'

'What makes you think that?' he cut in, his voice suddenly as curt as a whiplash.

'It all speaks for itself, doesn't it?' She gestured around her. 'This yacht—the way it's fitted out. It must have cost thousands. Naturalists don't earn that kind of money. I knew one when I was at university and he was as poor as a church mouse. Because he was a *real* naturalist, Mr Macrae—he *loved* animals. He didn't just use them, to make himself some kind of luxurious living, he——'

'Don't you think you're getting just a little muddled?' he demanded, and his eyes were like chips of ice now. 'First, I'm not a naturalist, naturalists don't earn the money I've obviously got, then I'm exploiting wildlife to make a living! You can't have it all ways, Alix my dear.'

'And I'm *not* your dear!' she flared at him. 'So just

keep your hands to yourself, give me back my passport
and let me go. I told you last night, I'm grateful for all
you've done, but I don't need any more help. I can
manage for myself from now on.'

'That's good news,' he drawled. 'But I think you'd
better have your breakfast first. It never does to decide
anything on an empty stomach.' Alix glanced at him
suspiciously and saw that his eyes were dancing, their
coldness gone, and she sighed with aggravation.
Frightening though his anger might be, she almost
preferred it to this patronising amusement. Not that it
mattered; she would soon be away and able to start
forgetting him.

Kinnan turned away and went down the steps into
the saloon and, after a moment's hesitation, Alix
followed him. He had fetched the coffee from the galley
when she ducked into the spacious cabin, and was
pouring out two mugs. Ungraciously, she accepted one
and sat down to drink it.

'Juice?' he offered. 'Rolls? Only a Continental
breakfast, I'm afraid, but I shouldn't think you're the
hearty eggs-and-bacon type anyway, are you? And
you'll be glad to hear I'm not, either—I'm rather keen
on muesli, as it happens, and always bring a big sack of
it with me whenever I sail.'

'How interesting,' Alix said coldly. 'But you're
wasting your time—I shan't be getting any breakfasts
for you, muesli or otherwise.'

'Well, of course not,' he agreed. 'I wouldn't expect
you to, I'm quite capable of looking after myself—
which makes two of us, doesn't it?' he added with a
disarming smile. 'No, Alix, all I want you to do is see
that the stores are kept up—not too difficult with the
market right there on the quay—and sort out some
kind of fairly substantial meal for the evening. Plus a
midday snack. I don't want a slave—not even a galley
slave.' He grinned. 'As I said before, I'll want you to

give a hand with some of the work for the film—which I *am* making, in spite of your doubts—and that involves coming out in the small boat with me while I make a couple of exploratory dives; nothing ambitious, diving isn't something one does alone. That's mainly why I need you, as a back-up in the very unlikely event of something going wrong.'

'But I wouldn't know what to do——' Alix began, and Kinnan interrupted her.

'I'd tell you. There's no need to worry—I wouldn't be doing anything dangerous. I intend to live a long time yet!'

There was a long pause. Almost without thinking, Alix took a roll and spread butter and cherry jam on it. She bit into it, realising how hungry she was. The coffee and the fresh orange juice were delicious and it was several minutes before she remembered that she hadn't intended eating anything.

'You will stay, Alix, won't you?' Kinnan said softly.

She looked at him and hesitated. Her heart fluttered suddenly, like a butterfly beating its wings against glass. The cabin seemed full of a strange tension, a tension she couldn't name. Kinnan's eyes met hers and she saw again that enigmatic expression that had bemused her earlier. She searched her mind for the doubts and arguments that had seemed so clear before, but they were muddled and confused. The tension was like a thread of spider's silk, stretching between them, holding them together, infinitely fine yet infinitely strong. She found herself unable to look away from the clear grey eyes and slowly, almost hypnotically, she nodded.

'Yes . . . I'll stay. But only for a few days,' she added quickly. 'Just until I get sorted out and you get your assistants. In any case, Bernie will probably be back soon and we'll be wanting to get on.'

'Ah yes,' he said. 'Bernie. . . .' And his eyes had an odd little gleam in them as he looked at her.

When she had finished eating, Kinnan took her
ashore. The market, which had started soon after six
that morning, was still thronged with people and Alix
would have liked to loiter, investigating the fruit and
vegetables for sale. But the thought of her lost luggage
reminded her that other matters were more pressing.
Apart from some change and two one-hundred-dinar
notes in her shoulder-bag, she had no money, and she
had no change of clothes at all.

The bus station was close to the harbour and they
were there in a few minutes. Kinnan quickly found the
'complaints office' and to Alix's relief its occupant
spoke English and soon understood the problem. But
that was as far as her good luck went; there had been
no trace of her rucksack, either at Dubrovnik or at
Mostar, where the bus had gone next, and it seemed
certain that some opportunist had quietly shouldered it
as he left the bus. Leaving me destitute, Alix thought
with a sudden feeling of terror. She had a vivid picture
of how lost and alone she would feel without Kinnan's
help and support, and her see-sawing emotions,
constantly swinging between resentment and gratitude,
veered once again, although she was still determined
that she would be on her way as soon as possible.

'Well, that seems to be that,' he remarked as they left
the noise and dust of the bus station and went back
towards the harbour. 'What now?'

'I don't know,' Alix said miserably, and he gave her a
sharp glance.

'A cup of coffee, I think,' he decreed, steering her
away towards the head of the harbour. 'Look ahead—
that's one of the Dubrovnik's biggest department
stores, and they have a rather nice roof restaurant. You
can see all over Gruz from there. We'll sort something
out up there.'

They chose a table at the side, looking over the
harbour. It certainly was beautiful, Alix thought, and

the weather was perfect. If only things hadn't started to go wrong. If only Bernie had never had to go back to England. . . .

'Now then,' Kinnan said firmly when the coffee arrived, 'let's start at the beginning. How much money do you have?'

'Not much,' she confessed. 'My travellers' cheques were all in my rucksack.'

'I see. But the bank must have given you some address or telephone number, in case you lost them.'

'Oh yes, so they did. But it wasn't here—it was in Belgrade. And I think there was one for Zagreb too. But the folder with all the information was——'

'In your rucksack,' he finished resignedly. 'All right, that's not an insuperable problem. We can probably get the information from a bank. I don't suppose it will take too long to get some money through to you. Have you got a note of the cheque numbers?'

'Yes,' said Alix in a low voice. 'But it's——'

'Don't tell me!' Kinnan's amusement began to give way to exasperation. 'Didn't it occur to you to keep these things separately? No, obviously it didn't. My God, you've got a lot to learn. Haven't you ever been abroad before?'

'Only once, on a school trip,' Alix retorted, her own anger beginning to rise again. 'Not all of us have had your advantages, remember. My parents had to work hard to bring me up. They made enough sacrifices just to get me through university. I didn't think it was necessary to ask for more so that I could have foreign holidays!'

His eyes narrowed. 'While I've spent all my formative years travelling the Continent and living in the lap of luxury, I suppose.'

'Well, haven't you?' she challenged.

'That isn't really your business,' he snapped, his good humour entirely gone now. 'You know, I'm beginning to wonder why I bother. You aren't exactly the easiest person in the world to help. So you don't have any record of the numbers and you don't know the telephone number. Well, at least we know where we have to start—right at the beginning.' He fished in his pocket and brought out a wallet. 'Look, you'd better go and get yourself some clothes while I go along to the bank and start off some enquiries. You can come along there to meet me in case they want your signature, or just come back to *Manta* if you're a long time.' He held out some notes. 'The bank's on the quay——'

'What are you talking about?' Alix stared at the notes. 'I can't take money from you!'

Kinnan sighed again. 'Why the hell not? You're supposed to be working for me, remember? So I'm paying you in advance, what's so wrong with that? Or you can consider it a loan if you must, but surely it makes sense to get yourself a few more clothes. You'll need a bit more than what you've got on. I suggest some shorts, a few tops and a bikini, unless you're keen on nude sunbathing.'

'I certainly am not!'

He grinned suddenly. 'Why ever not? The Yugoslavs are very keen on it—there are quite a few beaches set apart for naturists. And there's nothing wrong with it— perfectly wholesome and healthy, in fact I think personally there's no better way to enjoy the elements than in the natural state.'

'I'd rather stick to a bikini,' Alix said coolly. She hesitated. She certainly was going to need some more clothes—and if she could get her own money she would be able to repay Kinnan. Meanwhile she still needed his help, and if she could work to earn her keep maybe that was the best way. With a tiny shrug, she took the money. 'But I won't need all this much.'

'I'd appreciate it if you took it, all the same,' he told her. 'Get yourself a dress too.' But she shook her head firmly.

'I'll get what I need, thank you. And I'll give you back whatever's left.'

'Have it your own way,' he said, sounding bored suddenly. 'Now, let's get moving. You'll find all you need here, I should think—and I'll see you back on *Manta*. I can tell you what's happened at the bank then.'

Alix went down into the store to do her shopping. It didn't take long—a few of the assistants spoke English, but even if they hadn't it was easy enough to mime the actions of trying on and buying clothes. It was less than an hour before, equipped with shorts, a couple of T-shirts and suntops, a new rucksack, bikini and some underwear, she was back on board *Manta*, where Kinnan was sitting at the saloon table surrounded by papers and charts.

'They'll need your signature at the bank,' he said without looking up. 'We can go along later, they'll be closed during the hottest part of the afternoon. Get yourself equipped?'

'Yes, thank you.' She hesitated in the doorway, uncertain of what to do next. After a moment, Kinnan glanced up and said vaguely: 'Get a bit of lunch together, will you? You'll find everything you need in the galley—cold meat, cheese, a bit of salad, anything like that.' And when she still hesitated, he added curtly: 'Well? Suddenly lost the use of your limbs?'

Alix's cheeks flamed at his rudeness and she turned without a word and went into the galley. How dared he speak to her like that! As if she were some kind of servant—but then wasn't that just what she was? She bit her lip, her hazel eyes misting with tears. Yes, to Kinnan Macrae that obviously *was* all she was—a useful pair of hands, someone to wait on him and be a general dogsbody. And the worst of it was there was nothing she could do about it. She had accepted his help—and his money. She had agreed to work for him.

And until she'd earned at least the cost of the clothes he'd bought her, that was what she had to do.

Silently, she prepared a meal and took it through to the saloon. Kinnan grunted without raising his eyes from his work, and after a pause Alix took her own lunch up on deck. The sun was blazing down now; she found a patch of shade and settled down to eat.

But her thoughts were disturbing. Try as she might, she couldn't stop thinking of the man below. The memory of his kisses hovered at the edge of her mind, impinging on everything else, and she quivered as she remembered those moments when he had held her in his arms, his fingers and lips drawing from her a response she would never have believed possible—a response she had never known was possible. He had awakened sensations she had never before experienced; she was half excited, half frightened by them.

Alix had never been short of boy-friends. At university she had been one of a crowd of students, all visiting each other's rooms and treating each other with the easy familiarity of brothers and sisters. But there had nevertheless been a succession of boys who had wanted more; and in a few cases Alix herself had been aware of wanting more too. But she had never found it—until now. . . .

With a tiny crash, she set her orange-juice glass down on the deck. What was she doing—thinking? Kinnan Macrae was nothing to her—never could be, *mustn't* be. Those moments in his arms had proved nothing but the fact that he was, as she had first suspected, a womaniser, a playboy, taking pleasure where and when he found it. She had little option but to agree to his offer of a job, but that didn't mean she had to agree to anything else. And the fact that he had evoked such a response meant only that he was an expert, nothing more. And that he was dangerous.

She must be very careful not to let such a situation

arise again, Alix determined as she picked up her plate
and glass and went back to the saloon to collect
Kinnan's and wash up. In a way, it was just as well it
had happened—she knew now just what she had to
guard against.

And guard against it she would!

The sun grew very hot during the afternoon and she
was glad to stay below decks and put away the new
clothes she had bought that morning. She slipped into a
pair of white shorts and a brief yellow suntop, spent
some time cleaning the galley and getting to know the
equipment there, then wandered back into the saloon.

Kinnan glanced up from his papers, stretched and
yawned.

'Loose end?' he enquired, and Alix nodded.

'I wondered if there was anything you'd like me to
do.'

'No, I don't think so. I'll take you into the old city
later on—it's very interesting at night. Have you
explored the boat?'

'No, I didn't like to without asking you first.'

'I'll show you round,' he said, getting up. 'Just about
due for a breather anyway. Now, you know your own
cabin, just off the saloon; mine's on the starboard side.'
He opened the next door and she saw a small cabin,
exactly like her own yet unmistakably Kinnan's. The
same air of subtle luxury pervaded the small space, yet
everything was rugged, workmanlike—and expensive.

Kinnan glanced sideways at her, his eyebrows lifting
in a quirk of humour. 'Not exactly the setting for a
love-nest, is it? Such a narrow little bed. . . .'

Alix felt her face flame and turned away quickly.
Why must he always draw attention to the awareness
between them? Even now her skin was tingling as his
body brushed against hers in the narrow space. And she
knew that he was smiling as he closed the door.

'Two spare cabins,' he went on, opening doors briefly

to show her, and the forepeak, which I don't use as a cabin. I keep all my diving gear here.' He showed her the small, triangular room, its two berths merging under the bows and packed with gear Alix couldn't begin to recognise. She stared at it, picking out items that were vaguely familiar from TV programmes—wetsuits, snorkels, an aqualung. But most of it was beyond her, and she acknowledged that Kinnan hadn't been lying when he'd told her he was a serious diver.

'Meanwhile, back aft,' he continued, closing the door and leading her back through the saloon, 'we have the deckhouse, which you already know, and the aft cabin. Again, not a cabin in the usual sense of the word.' He unlocked the door and Alix peered into the most efficiently fitted out darkroom she had ever seen, with photographic equipment stored neatly in lockers and developing materials and film in sealed polythene boxes. She stared at it all, bemused. There must be thousands of pounds' worth here, she thought, and her original idea of Kinnan as a rich playboy, able to indulge any fancy, came back into her mind.

'Well?' he said when they were back in the galley and he was making iced drinks for them both. 'What do you think of it?'

Alix took the drink and shrugged, following him out to the deckhouse where he had erected an awning. 'All very lush. You must be very pleased with it.'

He glanced at her, grey eyes assessing. 'Do I detect a note of disapproval?'

'Disapproval?' Alix said tightly. 'Why should I disapprove? Who am _I_ to disapprove?'

'And now I know you do,' he remarked. 'That cool note in your voice, that studied indifference. But you're not indifferent to me, are you, Alix my dear? Disapproving or not, you're certainly not indifferent.' He reached out a lazy hand and, before she could move, caught her wrist. 'What is it? What don't you like about my boat—or about me?'

'I don't know what you're talking about,' she retorted, her heart pounding. 'You don't mean a thing to me—you or your boat. Oh, I admit I'm grateful for the help you've given me—quite frankly, I don't know how I'd have managed without it, though I suppose I would have somehow. But once I've got myself sorted out and you've got your assistants here—which I hope won't be too long—then I shall just go on with my holiday.'

'I see,' he murmured, and she was conscious of his fingers against the tender skin of her wrist, moving gently, almost caressing. 'Just an interlude. But a pleasant one, I'd like to think—not something to be simply dismissed from your mind as you shoulder your rucksack and wander off into the sunset.'

'That rather depends on you, doesn't it,' she snapped, and he raised one eyebrow enquiringly.

'It does? In what way?'

'Oh, for heaven's sake!' She pulled at his hand, trying to twist herself from his grasp, but his fingers were like steel. 'I should have thought that was obvious! Just leave me alone—let me get on with whatever it is you want me to do—and keep your *hands* off me! I can't stand being pawed!'

'Pawed, is it?' His voice hardened but he didn't let go. 'It didn't strike me that way earlier—didn't strike me you were all that keen to get away, either. In fact, if I'd been asked I'd have had to admit you seemed to enjoy it every bit as much as I did. So what's happened since then? I'll ask you again, Alix—just what is it about me you don't like?'

'All right, I'll tell you.' She was breathing hard, aware of every particle of his fingers around her wrist; aware of the bone and muscle, the warm, pulsing blood, the smooth, firm skin. Her fears returned in a rush.

This man spelt danger—she mustn't let him affect her like this, and if the only way to stop it was to make him angry. . . . She tilted her head back and looked up into his eyes, annoyance flaring in her as she caught their quizzical amusement.

'I'll tell you what I don't like. It's money—the smell of it, the signs of it. The whole place reeks of money, and so do you.' She glanced contemptuously down at his wrist, at the gold watch that encircled it. 'All this— this expensive yacht, the diving equipment, all that photographic gear—you must have spent a fortune, and not such a small one either. Oh yes, I believe you're what you say you are—a TV film-maker. But it's been easy for you, hasn't it? Money makes everything easier. You might not be so pleased with yourself if you'd had to work for it—if you hadn't had the money to set you up in the first place.'

He stared at her, his fingers tightening on her wrist until she wanted to cry out, but although she couldn't prevent the tears of pain coming to her eyes she continued to stare back at him, defiance in every quivering line of her.

'My God,' he said slowly. 'You really do have a chip on your shoulder, don't you? What happened to you— no silver spoon when you were a baby and you've resented it ever since? Or maybe Grandma left all her money to the cats' home, was that it? Though if that were the case I'm surprised you didn't get a hefty share!'

Even as the fury blazed through Alix her hand lifted and struck him hard across the cheek. It was almost as if she had stepped outside her body and was watching, detached, as he stared at her, raising his own free hand to touch the marks that scored first livid then scarlet across his tanned skin. His expression changed; the scorn to amazement, the amazement to a wrath that set her trembling. And then she was back inside her body with a bang as he jerked her towards him, one hand encircling two slender wrists, the other holding her slim body hard against his own. She could feel every line, every contour, from rigid leg muscles through taut thigh to a chest that was like a stone wall; a stone wall that held a heart like a bull, steadily battering at its enclosure as if determined to get out.

'That does it,' he growled, and his voice was like the snarl of a lion disturbed from its lair. 'You've been pushing your luck all day, young Alix, and now you've gone too far. You need a lesson, my lady, and I'm about to give it to you—a lesson you won't forget!'

Alix opened her mouth to make some angry retort, though her heart was thudding with terror. But before she could utter a sound his own mouth had taken possession of it, his lips harsh, crushing her own against her teeth so that she tasted blood, forcing her head back against the hand that was spread out behind it. His arm was like a steel bar, curving round her body and up between her shoulder blades, making it impossible for her to move; she was vibrantly aware of the hardness and sheer masculinity of his body, and her heart gave a wild kick of fear as he swung her easily into his arms and down the steps into the saloon.

As he laid her on the berth, her suntop caught in the edge of the table and ripped away. Alix gasped and twisted her body, trying to hide herself from his searching gaze, but again his strength prevented her from moving and she could only lie there and gaze helplessly up at him as his eyes moved slowly, caressingly, over her white breasts.

And then she was swept by a wave of desire that took her entirely by surprise as Kinnan bent his head to kiss her and his lips dragged, almost as if against his will, from her mouth down the column of her neck to the breast that his hand cupped as tenderly as if it were made of spun glass. Alix felt her own hands creep up the smooth skin of his back, felt the muscles tight and rippling under the surface, tangled her fingers in his thatch of hair. Hardly knowing what she did, she pressed his face closer against her own softness, glorying in the slight roughness of his chin against her silkiness, gasping with pleasure as he took a taut nipple between his teeth, worrying at it gently like a playful puppy. Sensuously, she moved her body on the berth, inviting him to come closer, and murmured his name as he stretched his length against her. All her fears were forgotten; as she returned kiss for kiss she knew that nothing else mattered but this; that Kinnan had become her world and that nothing must be allowed to come between them. Not even—and she shifted slightly as his hand slid down over her breasts to fumble with the fastening of her shorts—a scrap of cotton and lace. She wanted to feel him close against her; all of him; mouth to mouth, skin to skin, heart to heart.

Kinnan raised his head and looked down at her. His eyes, which could be ice or steel, were now smoky with desire, the misty grey of a summer morning that promises warmth and sunshine to come. They were grave and questioning as they searched her face, and she knew what he was asking her.

Alix took a deep breath and nodded. She wanted to speak, to say yes, please . . . but the words wouldn't come. Her own hazel eyes were almost green in the dim light of the cabin, and the answer they gave seemed to satisfy him, for he bent his head again and now there was a new purpose in his kisses.

It was only gradually that they realised there was someone else on board the ketch.

The slight rocking movement of the boat changed just perceptibly. Absorbed as they were in each other, their surroundings had faded; but they both noticed it, and their lovemaking stilled.

Dazed, hardly aware of where she was, Alix watched

as Kinnan lifted his head. A tiny frown gathered
between his brows and his eyes narrowed. Then a voice
called his name; with a sound that was half groan, half
oath, he jerked himself away from Alix and flung her
suntop over her. Still bewildered, half in a dream, she
fumbled to put it on. But she still wasn't quite covered
when the square of light from the hatchway darkened
and the newcomer peered in.

'Kinnan darling! So you *are* on board. I was
beginning to think the boat was deserted, it was so
quiet.' The figure came down the steps and stood there,
dark eyes taking in the scene. 'Dear me, I seem to have
interrupted something!'

Alix tugged the suntop into position and sat up,
staring at the woman who had just arrived. She was
tall—almost as tall as Kinnan—and undoubtedly
beautiful, with a cloud of thick black hair that curled
around her shoulders, the kind of hair that could never
be tamed but framed the sultry beauty of the full-lipped
face. She was deeply tanned and her voluptuous body,
shown off to perfection by the clinging jersey silk of the
lime green dress she wore, seemed to exude an aura of
sheer animal attraction; the kind of attraction that must
be felt by any male within five miles, Alix thought,
overwhelmed by the other girl's presence, by her sudden
and unexpected appearance, and by the abrupt
curtailment of what had promised to be the most
shattering experience of her life.

'Vita!' Kinnan exclaimed. 'How did you get here—
and why didn't you let me know you were coming?'

'No time, darling,' she drawled. 'I just got on a plane
and came. The grapevine said you needed an
assistant—and I rather jumped at it.' Her dark eyes slid
over Alix, almost contemptuously. 'Hope you don't
mind. It certainly seems as if you need someone.'

Alix felt her face flame at the implication behind the
words. Presumably this—this Vita, whoever she was,

thought that Alix was a local girl, picked up and brought here for an afternoon's dalliance. And presumably, she thought, a hard lump of misery settling in the pit of her stomach, Vita knew Kinnan well enough to realise that he was capable of doing such a thing. She was suddenly relieved that Vita had interrupted them. She had been about to give herself to a man who was nothing but a casual philanderer— something she had always sworn she would never do. Her fear of this man had been right, she realised. She had seen him for what he was and vowed to guard against her own body's betrayal, and she had forgotten that vow. Well, it wouldn't happen again!

'Excuse me,' she said, scrambling to her feet. 'There's something I have to do, I——'

She saw Vita's look of surprise as she realised that Alix was English, then Kinnan was in front of her, blocking her way.

'There's no need to go, Alix——'

'Please, I need to——'

'And especially not before I've introduced you,' he went on, ignoring her protests. 'Alix, this is Vita Purvis, a friend of mine. Vita, I want you to meet Alix Daley— my fiancée.'

A stunned silence followed his words. To Alix, it was as if the world had shifted, leaving her abandoned in space, falling with an abruptness that sickened her. Blindly she put out a hand and Kinnan caught and held it, his grasp warm and solid, bringing her back to earth. She blinked and looked at the other girl.

Vita was looking as stunned as Alix felt. Her eyes had narrowed and a hardness touched her full lips as she stared at them. Alix was aware of a malevolence, an almost tangible dislike, in the glance that the other girl gave her. In that moment, the voluptuous beauty showed her age, a good ten years more than Alix had at first supposed—almost the same age as Kinnan, she guessed. But the moment was gone as quickly as it came and she doubted if Kinnan had even registered it.

'Your *fiancée*?' The words came in a whisper, but Vita was already recovering her poise. 'Surely this is rather sudden?'

Kinnan acknowledged this with a nod. 'It did happen quite quickly,' he admitted, and Alix felt anger seethe within her as she recognised that tinge of humour in his voice. How dared he put her in this position and then laugh at her? How *dared* he?

'It may end just as quickly, of course,' she said sweetly, and Vita gave her a suspicious glance.

'Who can tell?' Kinnan cut in before she could speak. His tone was light but his eyes hard as he looked intently into Alix's eyes. 'At the moment, however, we're both very much in love—and hope things will stay that way, don't we, darling?'

Alix didn't reply. She was completely bemused. What was the relationship between Kinnan and Vita? She had spoken to him so possessively when she had arrived, sure of a welcome; the way a woman would speak to her lover, Alix thought, growing cold. And there was definitely a tension between them. Something more powerful than mere friendship existed between these two. But if that was the case, why had Kinnan introduced her as his fiancée? What possible motive could he have?

One thing was sure. Now that Vita had arrived, he wouldn't be wanting Alix aboard any longer. Somehow, she would have to find a way of leaving. Even if he did want her to stay, there could be no question of it now. There was more than one reason why she had to leave—and his effect on her wasn't the least of them.

Because she knew now that there was more than a physical attraction between them—on her side, at least. During those heady moments in his arms, when she would have sold the world for the completion of their lovemaking, there had been more than desire surging through her body, more than sheer animal excitement, more than passion. There had been love. And when the rest had died away, banished by the appearance of the other girl, love had remained. And, she knew, always would remain.

Why had she ever had to get into this mess? she thought despairingly. A chain of circumstance—if she hadn't gone to the police station when she did, if she hadn't lost her rucksack, if Bernie hadn't had to go back to England. . . .

If she'd never come to Yugoslavia in the first place.

CHAPTER FOUR

It was some time before Alix could speak to Kinnan alone.

There was, it seemed, too much to discuss. Why Vita had come; who else was flying out to take the place of Kinnan's injured assistants, who had now arrived in England and were being treated in hospital. Much of the talk went over Alix's head, consisting as it did of names that meant nothing to her. But she tried to listen in the hope that she might gain some clue to Kinnan's behaviour and to his relationship with Vita.

'So young Jon Redmond's coming to help with the camera work,' he remarked, handing them both iced drinks. 'Well, I've no objection to that. I've thought for some time I'd like to work with him, especially as he dives well too. When is he likely to arrive?'

'In two or three days,' Vita replied, her dark eyes resting on him with a secret, enigmatic look. 'I took the opportunity to come ahead, since there wasn't much doing for me on the paper. Thought there might be a story in the hold-up.'

Kinnan nodded. 'Vita's a journalist,' he told Alix. 'You've probably read some of her features—she writes for one of the big dailies and a couple of glossies.'

'Yes, I have,' said Alix, realising now why the name had seemed vaguely familiar. 'You did a feature on arranged marriages a little while ago.'

'One of my hobbyhorses,' Vita smiled. 'It's very interesting when you look into it deeply and see just how often these arranged marriages work. It certainly makes you wonder about old-fashioned romance—after all, once the rosy tint has worn off your spectacles, life can seem very plain and bare if you have nothing else in common.'

'But does it have to wear off?' Alix asked. 'And would it be there anyway if a couple *didn't* have anything in common?'

Vita's smile widened. 'Wherever did you find her?' she asked, turning to Kinnan with an indulgent chuckle. 'Such refreshing naïvety! It seems almost sad that she'll learn, just like the rest of us. But the sooner the better, I'm afraid, or you'll be badly hurt, my child,' she added, turning back to Alix. 'However, I'm sure you can trust Kinnan to see that it's not *too* badly. No—my researches into arranged marriages didn't convince me at all about love at first sight being the only thing. After all, life is so material these days that it seems only common sense to base the most important relationship of life on a similar foundation. Of course, if there's physical attraction as well, one then has the best of all worlds.'

Her eyes returned to Kinnan, smouldering, almost devouring, and Alix felt her cheeks burn. She would be a fool not to know what Vita was driving at, she thought. The message was loud and clear. Love wouldn't enter into Vita's scheme of life—material considerations certainly would. And Kinnan's material assets, combined with his physical ones, made a very attractive package indeed—and one that Vita was determined to retain for herself. In other words, keep off the grass.

'By the way,' Vita remarked almost without pausing, 'I haven't seen your engagement ring yet. Perhaps you don't wear it about the boat—wise, I'm sure, but surprising in such a romantic. Pop along and slip it on for me to see, there's a sweet.'

Agonisedly, Alix glanced at Kinnan, but he didn't flicker an eyelid. Easily, stretching out his long tanned legs, he said: 'We haven't got around to that yet, Vita. I told you, it happened rather suddenly. But I mean to take Alix into the old city at the first opportunity and choose something really special for her.' He swung his feet to the deck before Vita, looking put out, could speak, and went on casually: 'We'd better get along to the bank now, Alix. I've a notion there might be some hold-up in that business of yours and I'd like to get it sorted out soon, so that we can go off to the island tomorrow as arranged and do that preliminary diving.' He smiled at Vita. 'Sorry we can't ask you along too, but the dinghy will be loaded up as it is, you know how much equipment's needed. Anyway, you're not keen on boats, are you?'

And who should *that* round be scored to? Alix thought as she followed Kinnan ashore, all too conscious of Vita's look of scorching dislike directed at her shoulder blades. Vita—or Kinnan? Certainly not to her—she seemed to be a pawn in some mysterious mental battle that was going on between them, and of no more interest than that to either of the protagonists.

Or was she wrong about that too?

Kinnan was striding ahead, his legs long and athletic in the faded denim shorts. He didn't seem interested in whether Alix was there or not; and then he turned, smiled at her and, as she came up to him, slipped an arm about her shoulders.

Alix's heart leaped. Then she caught the direction of his gaze and realised that this must be for Vita's benefit. Chilled, she drew away.

'Hullo,' he drawled, 'blowing cold again, are we?'

'Nothing of the sort. I just don't like being used.'

'Used?'

'As some kind of bargaining counter with your girl-friend. Oh, you needn't deny it—it's obvious by the way she looks at you. What I don't understand is why you told her we were engaged. Are you trying to make her jealous, or something? Because I tell you, Kinnan, I don't intend to play games with you or anyone else—as soon as we get back to the boat I shall collect my things and go, and you can tell Vita what you like. It won't interest me, because I won't be here!'

'Go?' he echoed. 'But we've had all that out before, Alix. You're staying—for a while, at least. You agreed, remember? And I still need your help.'

'No, you don't. Not now she's here.'

Kinnan threw back his head and laughed. 'And can you really see Vita Purvis cooking the supper—or acting as dogsbody while I do some preliminary dives? Because I can't! No, I still need you, Alix, believe me— more than ever, if truth be known.'

'Because there are two of you to cook for now?' Alix countered. 'Well, I never did think you saw me as anything more than a servant. And at least I suppose now she's here you won't want me to satisfy your— your lust!'

Kinnan raised his brows in the way she found so maddening—and so attractive.

'Strong words, my lady! Lust, is it? And was that what it was to you too?'

His tone was deceptively gentle, and Alix had opened her mouth to say no when she realised that she couldn't. He mustn't know the truth—that she had fallen in love with him. If he did, he would have complete power over her—and there was no way she could face that.

'I suppose it must have been,' she muttered, and he smiled.

'Missing Bernie, hm?' he murmured insinuatingly. 'Well, Alix, my dear, don't let it worry you. We'll have plenty of opportunity to be alone—and I'll guarantee you won't be missing your boy-friend once we've completed what we began earlier. In fact, you might even be glad he had to go back to England.'

Alix felt trapped. She'd deliberately allowed Kinnan

to assume Bernie was her boy-friend and that they were sleeping together, thinking it would keep her safe from him. Now it seemed that all she had achieved was to convince him that she was as promiscuous as he obviously was, glad of any chance encounter; he might just have respected her virginity before, but now there was no chance. And her response to him on the occasions when he had held her in his arms—especially that last occasion—would only reinforce that view.

'I'm sorry,' she said coldly. 'You seem to have got the wrong idea. I'm not about to complete anything—in fact my experience so far only makes me think it wouldn't be worth completing! It was all right as far as it went, but I was getting pretty bored by the time Vita turned up. You're no great shakes as a lover, Kinnan Macrae, or hasn't anyone ever told you that? Maybe the others were all too bemused by your money to mention it. I'm not!'

Kinnan stopped in his tracks. She could see that she had angered him and she felt her knees weaken, recalling his reaction the last time. But they were on the main road, in full view of yachts, shops and offices. She could see him grinding his teeth with frustration, and then he said in a voice that was more of a snarl:

'You'll regret having said that, Alix Daley. If I have to hold you on my boat by force, you'll take every last syllable back before I've done with you. So you're the big expert on love—well, I'll show you a few things you maybe aren't quite so expert on. Who knows, it might even help you to grow up!'

'You'll show me nothing,' she retorted, standing her ground though it seemed to be shaking beneath her. 'Because I'm not going to be around to *be* shown. I told you, I'm leaving—and you can't stop me!'

'Can't I?' he gritted. 'Maybe you've forgotten whose clothes you're wearing! Try to leave and I'll give myself the pleasure of reclaiming every stitch myself. And there's one other thing you've forgotten, little Miss Muffet—I've still got your passport! And that's something you won't leave without—and something you won't get back till I'm good and ready to give it to you!'

Alix stared at him, her heart sinking. She had indeed forgotten all about her passport. The trap seemed to be closing around her. Whichever way she turned, another door closed.

'Now let's understand each other,' he went on, his voice still a low, angry growl. 'You carry out the terms of our bargain. You stay with me on *Manta*, doing the job you agreed to do, until I don't need you any more. That pays for your clothes, your keep, and anything you may earn over and above that. And you go on acting as my fiancée. I've got very good reasons for requiring that—reasons that are in your interests as much as mine.'

'What—reasons?' she whispered, her voice dry and husky.

'I've a good mind not to tell you, but I suppose I'd better. Vita's a journalist, as I told you, a feature-writer. What I didn't tell you—because she doesn't realise I know—is that she also contributes to the gossip column of the daily she writes for. Now, this may not matter to you, since you're so experienced in the ways of the world—but do you really want to feature in the gossip column of one of Britain's leading papers? Sunning yourself in Yugoslavia's nudist paradise with Kinnan Macrae aboard his luxury yacht, that kind of thing? Or maybe it's just the kind of publicity you'd love!'

Alix closed her eyes. Now she knew that there was definitely, finally, no way out of the trap. Kinnan had caught her as surely as he might have hooked an innocent fish, too unknowing to do other than to take the bait. He was right; she dared not let her name get into the gossip column of Vita's newspaper. It was the paper her own parents read; she could not let them open it one morning to find her name emblazoned across the page, to read a story that could not fail to hurt and upset them. Even now, Vita might well report the so-called engagement—though that, although it might surprise her parents, would not affect them in the same way that the news of their daughter apparently living a reckless life abroad certainly would. She would have to go along with it, at least until she could get away and sort things out properly again.

Kinnan was watching her.

'Well?'

'All right. You win.' Her voice sounded tired. 'I'll go along with you. There are—people I wouldn't want to see any gossip about me.'

' "People" meaning Bernie, I guess,' he said with an edge of bitterness to his voice. 'I must meet this young man some time. I'm interested to see just what impressive qualities he has. Well, enough of that.' He began to walk towards the bank. 'Let's get this money business settled. I've got a lot of work to do, and so far none of this is helping much.'

Alix followed him, her shoulders drooping with depression. The last exchange between them seemed to have left her in a greater muddle than ever. And just at that moment, she couldn't see any possible way out.

The rest of the day passed in what was for Alix a strained atmosphere. Having apparently satisfied himself that he had subdued both his women, Kinnan was at his most urbane, treating them both with a courtesy that plainly maddened Vita as much as it did Alix. But Vita seemed to be more efficiently armoured against it; although her smouldering eyes were a clear indication of her mood, she continued to behave in a proprietorial and seductive way, treating Kinnan like a lover whose momentary straying was nothing more than a cause for indulgent amusement. Like a mother, punishing her small boy for some prank while looking forward to recounting his misdeeds to her friends, Alix thought. Maybe it even excited her, increased Kinnan's masculinity in her eyes. Whatever the truth, the older girl certainly didn't seem too upset by his engagement. She must feel very secure indeed.

In the evening, Kinnan took them both to dinner at the yacht marina. It was pleasant but rather characterless. Alix had been looking forward to going into the old city and wondered why Kinnan had brought them here, then comforted herself with the reflection that she would rather postpone her introduction to the old city until Vita wasn't with them. In any case, she wasn't very interested in her food and toyed with it, glad when Kinnan took them back to *Manta* and mixed a final drink.

'Dear old *Manta*,' Vita said affectionately, stroking the teak coaming as they sat under the stars. 'We've had some good times in her, haven't we, Kinnan?'

'Very good,' he agreed.

Vita lay back, stretching her arms above her head to reveal the full, curving lines of her figure. 'The Mediterranean ... Greece ... Italy ... so many memories. And now the Adriatic. You certainly understand the way to live, Kinnan darling.'

Yes, Alix thought. The hedonistic way to live. Enjoying yourself, money no object. Swimming, diving, photography in the clearest and warmest waters on earth. Making a living, yes, and a fat one too, but still by doing all the things other people must pay to do for recreation.

How could she have fallen in love with such a man? When all her life had been geared to respect for hard work and care with money? When she had seen, painfully and tragically, just what too much money could do. . . .

Quietly she slipped down into the saloon and made

her way to her cabin. Where Vita was to sleep she neither knew nor cared. For form's sake, presumably it would be one of the spare cabins. In fact, she had more than a suspicion that it would be Kinnan's. And the thought brought an added heaviness to the misery that already sat like lead in her stomach.

The next morning was bright and warm. Alix woke early and, remembering her duties, was at the market on the quay soon after six, buying fresh fruit and vegetables with the money Kinnan had given her for housekeeping—or boatkeeping, he'd added with a smile. It had been one of their rare relaxed moments together, when Alix had felt no need to be on the defensive, and she wished they could come more often. Not very likely, especially now that Vita had joined them, and she took her time over the rest of her shopping for bread, cheese and meat, wanting to delay her return to *Manta*.

However, Vita was nowhere to be seen when she did return, and Kinnan was already drinking his coffee and glancing at his watch when Alix ducked down into the saloon with her loaded basket.

'Ah, there you are. Coffee? Get that lot put away as quickly as you can, will you, and knock up some sort of packed lunch. I want to get going as soon as possible. Gets too hot to do much later in the day, so I want to make the most of the morning. Better bring a long-sleeved shirt with you if you're still liable to burn, too.'

'I haven't got one,' Alix told him in dismay. 'I only bought sleeveless things.'

Kinnan sighed. 'You'd better have one of mine, then. I told you not to skimp!' He disappeared into his cabin, closing the door behind him, and emerged a few moments later with a white shirt.

Alix began to prepare a picnic lunch. 'Where are we going?' she ventured, wondering if Vita were coming too.

'A small island offshore. Not very far—about a quarter of an hour in the motor-boat. It's near a bigger island called Lokrum, which is a delightful place but will be swarming with people on a day like this. Our island isn't visited by many people and we should have it more or less to ourselves.' He glanced at the preparations she was making. 'You don't need to put in enough for an army, there'll only be the two of us. It's not Vita's idea of a day out, and in any case she's doing a travel feature for one of her magazines and has to do some research on that today.'

'I see.' Her heart jumped at the thought of a whole day in Kinnan's company. She was only surprised that Vita was apparently content to let Kinnan go off for the day without her. But maybe, she thought wryly, the other girl knew that she had nothing to worry about— maybe she was that sure of him.

That was if anyone ever could be that sure of Kinnan Macrae. Alix glanced covertly at him and wondered if it were possible. That waving auburn hair; the tanned face against which his grey eyes were clear as the Adriatic itself; the strong features and determined jaw. Could anyone ever be sure of a man who looked like that? A man who was so clearly following his own path through life, who was so obviously accustomed to getting whatever he wanted? A tiny shiver ran through Alix's body. Yesterday, for a moment, she had thought that he wanted her, and she had been more than willing to give him what he desired. They had been interrupted then; but who was to say that today, alone together on some deserted island far from any other distraction, he wasn't going to carry out his threat and complete what had been started? Wasn't she being just plain crazy to go with him?

Probably, she conceded. But what choice did she have? He'd made it clear that theirs was an employer-employee relationship, whatever he'd told Vita, and

until she had earned enough to pay her way—and until
he chose to return her passport—she had to do as she
was told. And forewarned is forearmed, she reminded
herself. She'd had enough warnings where Kinnan
Macrae was concerned—surely she could make sure
that nothing else happened.

Of course she could . . . provided her own treacherous
senses didn't betray her!

The short trip out to the island in the motor-boat
that acted as *Manta*'s runabout did a good deal to
restore Alix's equilibrium. The beauty of the scenery as
they left the harbour and headed out through
Dubrovacka Inlet held her spellbound, and she gasped
with delight at the sight of Kolocep Island with its trees
and sandy coves. Then they rounded the Lapad
Peninsula and came within sight of Lokrum, and once
again the sight of the island, green with its thick
covering of trees that came almost down to the water,
filled her with pleasure.

'It looks so pretty and peaceful,' she said longingly as
they swept past the shores. 'I'd love to explore it.'

'No reason why you shouldn't some time,' Kinnan
answered laconically. 'It's a popular place—you can get
a boat from the old harbour, they run about every half-
hour. Got quite a lot going for it too—botanical
gardens, quite a good little museum—it's got a history
of its own; Richard the Lionheart was shipwrecked
here. Fantastic air scented with cypresses, and a couple
of nice beaches. One for nudists, like I mentioned
before. Not sandy beaches, incidentally—flat rock
counts as beach here, and it's better in my view. Water's
deep straightaway too—none of this wading for miles
to get it above your knees, you can dive straight in.'

'Sounds idyllic,' Alix said dreamily, thinking of long
days spent stretched out under the sun, with an
occasional dip to cool off. She might even change her
ideas about nude sunbathing and swimming too—but

she wasn't going to admit as much to her present companion. That would be asking for trouble! 'Where is it we're heading?'

'Straight ahead,' he answered, and she turned her eyes away from Lokrum. 'Little gem is what its Yugoslav name means—and it's a very appropriate one. Looks just like a jewel there in the sunlight, doesn't it?'

'Yes, it does,' she said softly, gazing at the tiny islet they were fast approaching. 'An emerald—set in turquoise. I don't think I've ever seen anything more beautiful.'

The islet did indeed look like a precious stone, the green of its cypress woods dark and mysterious against the sparkling blue of the Adriatic. Above, the azure sky hung like an upturned crystal bowl, shimmering in the heat. White rocks and sand fringed the island like porcelain, lapped with the lace of delicately breaking waves.

'Why does nobody come here?' Alix asked, her voice hushed, as Kinnan swung the boat into a minute harbour and chose a spot for his anchorage before turning off the engine.

The sudden silence caught her by surprise. She wasn't even sure she wanted him to answer, to break it, and it was a moment or two before he did.

'It's a nature reserve. You have to have a special permit, and they're not easy to get unless you have genuine scientific reasons for wanting to come. My film-making's acceptable, in fact they're delighted with it, and that's good for me too as it means they'll probably buy the film when it's finished. And just at the moment I happen to know that nobody else has a permit—so there'll be just the two of us here. All day,' he added with a drawl, and turned his gaze full on her.

Alix felt her heart stop, then kick with a sudden excitement and fear. Only the two of them! What chance did she have? She felt her body quiver as he came nearer and put one finger under her chin so that she was forced to meet his eyes. He let his other hand trail burning fingertips down her neck and into the collar of her shirt ... and then he moved away.

'Not the time for those lessons I promised you,' he murmured silkily. 'Not just yet. But it will come, little Alix, never you fear. It'll come. ... And now,' he went on, suddenly brisk, while Alix tried to regain control of breathing that seemed suddenly to have become ragged and painful, 'we must get down to work. First, let me tell you what I want you to do. I want to make a fairly short and shallow dive from the boat just here—just to see what there is down there, though the water's so clear you can almost tell without going into it. However, that is an illusion—you can always see more from below. Now, you've got to control things up here and keep an eye on me while I'm down—and this is for serious, remember. It's not usually a good idea to dive alone and I may have to rely on your help if anything goes wrong, understand?'

Alix nodded. She was beginning to wish she'd never agreed to this. It sounded as if Kinnan would be relying on her to a degree that was totally beyond reason. How would she know what to do if anything went wrong? She probably wouldn't even know it *had* gone wrong! Grim stories about divers suffering from 'bends' and having to be kept for hours, even days, in decompression chambers, came half-remembered into her mind. And divers running out of air—caught in rocks—attacked by some fearsome underwater creature. She looked at Kinnan with wide eyes and he grinned suddenly.

'Don't look so terrified! Nothing *is* going to go wrong. I'm not going deep enough to get decompression problems and you'll be able to see me almost all the time. I just want to have a look, get some idea of good sites for photography and that sort of thing. O.K.? Now, you can give me a hand getting kitted up. It takes quite a while!'

And no wonder, Alix thought after she had helped him array himself in facemask, snorkel tube, fins, B.C.D. (which she would have simply called a lifejacket) and aqualung. Not to mention the watch, depth gauge and compass which encircled his arm, the weightbelt that fastened round his waist and the knife and torch he carried as well.

'You'll sink like a stone,' she observed when he was ready. 'And why do you need a torch? You can see the sunlight on the bottom.'

'True. But that bottom you can see so clearly is about twenty feet down, and there are a lot of little nooks and crannies that won't be getting any light. I want to see what's there.' He sat on the side of the boat, his back to the water. 'Now, remember all I told you and don't worry—I don't intend to stay down long. But keep an eye on me, and be ready if I give the emergency signal, O.K.?' He settled the face-mask into position, winked at her through it and toppled over backwards into the water.

Alix peered down after him. He was swimming almost lazily, his feet in their black rubber fins moving slowly to control his progress as he drifted along, peering at clumps of seaweed or rock, investigating the deeper stretches that showed dark against the sun-dappled stones of the rest of the seabed. As he had promised, he never went completely out of sight, but as he moved slowly away from the boat Alix had to strain her eyes to keep him in view.

Comforted by his evident confidence, she relaxed a little. It certainly was perfect here, she thought dreamily. Absolutely quiet except for birdsong from the trees that fringed the little island, and the soft kiss of the waves on the rocky shore. Peaceful; idyllic. An island made for love.

She could see Kinnan, drifting along beneath the water like a great golden-brown fish. His chestnut hair flowed out behind his head; he looked like a merman, powerful and mysterious. She thought of Matthew Arnold's tragic poem of the merman, forsaken by his earthly mistress, the 'sand-strewn caverns, cool and deep, where the winds are all asleep'. It was another world down there, and Kinnan was a part of it. And suddenly, urgently, she longed to be part of it too. To be part of any world that was Kinnan's; to be part of his world. . . .

The water splashed and glittered in the sunlight as Kinnan's head broke surface a few feet from the boat. He shook back his hair, the water drops flying, and his teeth flashed white against his tan. Then, with a powerful stroke or two, he was beside the boat and climbing in over the stern.

'That was great,' he panted as Alix began to help him divest himself of his diving gear. 'There's a canister of fresh water there, look, use it to rinse the equipment while I write up my log. Everything, B.C.D. and all, there's a good girl.'

'Was it successful?' Alix asked, doing as she was told.

'Mm. Might even take you down for a few minutes later on, just to show you the sights. If you're good.' His glance rested on her for a moment and Alix felt herself flush. Good? What did he mean by that? 'Make sure you get all the salt off,' he added tersely, and she turned back to her task, her cheeks burning now for a different reason.

Why did he always have to spoil things? Just as they began to develop some kind of rapport, out he would come with some curt remark that left her feeling humiliated. She rinsed his fins in a resentful silence. The loveliness, the peace and the beauty of their surroundings seemed to have dimmed.

After a while Kinnan looked up from what he was doing and announced that it was time for lunch. Alix unpacked the food she had brought—ham, cheese, fresh bread, tomatoes and peaches—and they took it ashore in the small inflatable dinghy to eat, sitting on the flat rocks in the shade of a spreading cypress and gazing at the water. It was utterly quiet now; even the birds seemed to be enjoying a siesta, and Alix found herself growing sleepy, her eyelids drooping against the strong light of the sun.

'Lie back for a minute,' said Kinnan from behind her, where he was already stretched out on his back, his head resting on a folded towel. 'I don't intend to move for a while.' He spread one arm wide and moved it invitingly.

Not on your life, Alix thought, every instinct immediately on guard. Oh, she'd lie back, yes—maybe even doze for a few minutes. But rest her head on that muscular arm—let her body, almost naked in the bikini he'd paid for, rest close to that powerful brown torso, those long hard legs—that was out of the question. And the shiver of excitement that ran through her as she contemplated it only increased her caution.

Instead, she lay down on her own towel a few feet away. She stared up through the dark green of the cypress needles to the blue sky that showed patchily above. The soft lap of the water against the rocky shelf they lay on was as gentle and tranquillising as the tick of the bedroom clock. In a few moments, she was asleep.

She woke to find herself alone, and raised herself on one elbow to look for Kinnan. There was no sign of him at first—and then, after a moment or two, she saw him, standing some distance away at the edge of the rocks.

He was about to dive into the water. And Alix had stared at him for several moments, taking in every detail of his suntanned litheness, before it dawned on her that he was naked.

She lay down again at once. How *could* he—

when he knew that she was there, might wake at any moment and see him? Was it that he just didn't care—or, more likely, was it a streak of exhibitionism? All right, he had a fine body, perfectly proportioned, magnetically attractive. Did he have to keep bringing it to her notice? And he knew exactly what effect it had on her, too, she thought ruefully. He was all too well aware of the response that his touch evoked, had been alive to every tremor when he held her in his arms. Had told her, too, that he meant to teach her a lesson before they were through, and it didn't take much imagination to know just what form that lesson would take. As far as Kinnan Macrae was concerned, there was only one thing a man would be interested in teaching a woman. And that wouldn't be so bad if love came into it—but it didn't. She knew that. In Kinnan's view it would be an enjoyable interlude—and completely loveless.

If she were another kind of girl, perhaps it could be just as enjoyable for her too. But she wasn't. To her, sex had to mean love—and without it there could be only unhappiness and shame.

Kinnan had dived by now, a perfect, arching dive, entering the water with scarcely a splash. He had disappeared from view, the surface of the water close to the shore being out of Alix's sight. She sat there, arms wrapped round her knees, thinking how much she would enjoy a swim now—and how impossible it would be to go for one. At least while Kinnan was there.

'Penny for them?'

The voice, coming from behind her, startled her so much that she jumped like a cat, whipping round to stare up at the face twitching with amusement above the wet body that gleamed as if it was polished teak. Kinnan's eyes danced as he moved past her for his towel, and as he began to dry himself she realised bemusedly that he was once again wearing the brief blue swimming trunks he'd used that morning.

'I thought—I thought you were——' She gestured towards the sea and he chuckled.

'So you saw me? I was. Had a final dive and got out farther down, so as not to offend your maidenly susceptibilities.' His smile widened. 'You ought to have a dip yourself, it's wonderful in.'

'I was just thinking I'd like one,' she admitted.

'Go on, then. And take my advice and go *au naturel*, there's nothing like it, and it saves drying your swimsuit afterwards!' His finely-chiselled lips twitched again as he glanced down at her and added gravely: 'I won't look.'

'No, thank you,' Alix replied with dignity. 'I'm quite happy as I am.' She stood up and began to walk across the rocks.

'Swim out to the boat when you're ready,' he called after her. 'I want to go round into one of the other bays for another dive.'

The water was just cool enough to be refreshing after the heat of the sun, and Alix was strongly tempted to take Kinnan's advice and slip out of her bikini to feel its silkiness against the whole of her body. But he was already loading the small inflatable dinghy ready to return to the motor-boat. Resisting the impulse, she swam out ahead of him and had scrambled aboard before he arrived. And that was another danger point safely avoided, she thought, imagining him helping her aboard.

The second dive was to take place in a small cove on the other side of the island, out of sight of land and even more secluded than the tiny harbour. They went through the same procedure as before, and when he had finished and was back aboard, Kinnan glanced at her with a challenge in his eyes and said: 'Well? Ready for your own first dive?'

'Me?' Alix felt a mixture of excitement and apprehension bubble up inside her. 'But I don't know

anything about it—I might do something wrong—
I——'

'You can swim well enough,' he told her. 'And I'll be
with you. It'll only be for a few minutes, anyway, just to
give you an idea.'

'Well——' she said dubiously, and he nodded as if it
were settled.

'Good. Let's get you kitted up.' He had brought
everything necessary, she noticed with an increasing
sense of doom, and she had a wild desire to refuse, to
say it wasn't possible—but she could think of no reason
that he would accept. He'd seen her swim, he knew that
she'd expressed interest earlier. Any excuse would be
dismissed as pure cowardice—and she wasn't going to
allow him that pleasure. It might even be what he was
hoping for!

'All right,' she said with a firmness she was far from
feeling. 'I'm ready!'

'Good.' His grey eyes assessed her. 'I'm not going to
ask you to use an aqualung, don't worry—this is just a
snorkel dive. And you won't be going very deep, only a
few feet. But you'll be amazed at what you can see—
even with water this clear it's far more than when you
simply look down from above. Now, there are just a
few things to remember: you're going down on an
ordinary breath, so you won't be able to stay down any
longer than you would if you were just swimming as
you were just now. What you *can* do is use that time
more effectively because the fins will help you go deeper
and faster, and the mask will help you to see more
clearly. Right? Don't take too deep a breath, by the
way—you may hyper-ventilate and pass out. And if you
feel pressure in your ears, at about six feet, clear them
by pinching your nose. When you come up, make sure
there's nothing above you, and when you reach the
surface and want to breathe tip your head forward
again to clear the tube.'

'Yes, I see,' Alix said.

'You're not wearing a wetsuit,' Kinnan went on, as impartial now as if he were instructing a class of beginners, 'but you still need a lifejacket, so that goes on next. Right. Then the fins and weightbelt.' His fingers were cool against her skin as he adjusted the various harnesses and fastenings. 'I should think that will be about right. Now, I'm coming in too, but I'll be staying on the surface, so you can keep an eye on me if you feel nervous. And don't worry,' he added, fastening his own face mask, 'I'll be keeping an eye on you too!'

Alix repressed a nervous desire to giggle. They must look like a couple of men from Mars, she thought as she lowered herself gingerly into the water and swam a little way from the boat. Now that the moment had come, she felt oddly scared—yet, as Kinnan had explained, it was little more than the kind of duck-diving she often did while swimming. But there was more to it than that, she thought, taking a deep breath and then another before the breath that would take her under. It was as if everything that happened today was imbued with a special significance—as if it was all leading on to something else, something that would affect, or even change, her whole life. . . .

And then she was under and mentally gasping with delight at the underwater world. It seemed impossible that it could be there, separated from her world by water alone—it was so different, so entirely strange, so alien and so incredibly beautiful. Kinnan had been right: you did see more when you were actually a part of it than when you just peered down from above. She flicked her feet and the fins drove her down; as pressure built up in her ears she remembered his advice and pinched her nose and blew gently to clear them. A shoal of small fish drifted past ahead of her, followed by a larger one; on the floor of the sea, just below, she could see a crab making its way between the rocks, and the chrysanthemum shapes of anemones, crimson and gold, their fronds waving delicately as they searched blindly for passing food.

It was time to surface and she had only just begun to look! Reluctantly, she glanced up to make sure she wasn't under the boat, and saw Kinnan's body, oddly elongated, just above her. With a kick of her fins, she let herself float up to him. The weightbelt had been perfectly adjusted to give her neutral buoyancy; any movement was up to her. It took only one more flick to bring her to the surface and she even remembered to roll her head forward so that she could continue to breathe through the tube, before she gave Kinnan a beaming smile and began to take deep breaths for her next dive.

'Hey, hold it a moment!' He was laughing and holding her by the shoulders. 'Am I to take it you enjoyed it?'

'It was glorious!' she told him excitedly, lifting her mask. 'I've never seen anything like it—the colours, you'd never dream—and the fish and the rocks, and the beautiful seaweeds. Oh, and I saw anemones, huge ones, and a sea-urchin, all spiny like a hedgehog, and—oh, I don't know what else. There just wasn't enough *time*!'

'Not enough time, eh?' he teased her. 'So you'll be wanting an aqualung next, will you? To give you more time?'

'Oh *yes*,' she breathed, and lifted her face to his. Her eyes glowed green, taking their colour from the translucent sea around them, her face gleamed with water and sun, and radiated enthusiasm. For a long moment, their glances caught and held; then, just as Alix began to feel breathless, a wave rocked them together and she felt his arms slip round her shoulders to draw her closer. And although their lifejackets formed an effective barrier, below the water their legs met and entwined as above their mouths touched and merged.

The kiss was long and tender. Alix felt Kinnan's lips move gently over hers, his teeth making tiny nips in the soft flesh. One hand had slid down her back to caress her smoothly rounded flanks; she felt his fingertips against her thigh and knew a piercing delight as his legs gripped hers with an urgency that had her heart beating wildly against her ribs.

Then a small wave broke over their faces and they came apart, laughing tremulously. Kinnan kept his hands on her shoulders and watched her as she brushed a hand across her face; her mask had been knocked aside when he had first drawn her to him, and now, with shaking fingers, she attempted to readjust it.

'Let me.' His fingers steady, he put the mask right and then looked at her gravely. 'You're going down again?'

She nodded. There was nothing she wanted more at that moment than to go back into his arms, to repeat the experience they had just shared. But the moment had gone; she was no longer sure of herself, still less of him. It had been a reaction only, she told herself as she turned her body upside down and made her second exploration of that strange green world with its wavering light, its softened outlines and its brilliant, exotic life-forms—plants that looked like animals, animals that looked like plants. Her reaction to the man who had given her this new world; his to a girl who had let down all her defences in the enthusiasm of discovery. It meant no more than that.

But, after the diving was over and they had returned to the boat to rinse off their gear, stow it tidily away and make the trip back to Gruz, she knew that her instincts had once more proved right. She had known that if she didn't get away from Kinnan in the early stage of their relationship she would never be free of him. And she had known that everything that happened today was of some significance, pointing to a change in her life that would reverberate into old age.

If only she had followed those instincts, she thought as with an ache in her heart she watched the sunset turn the old city of Dubrovnik into a fortress of fire, its walls stained crimson and ruby in the glowing light. For even if she never saw Kinnan again after this moment, she would never be free of him; she would carry him for ever in her heart. And it was as if their kiss had sealed that knowledge, bringing it home to her in a way that perhaps nothing else could have done. It had been a moment out of time; a moment in which they had both hung, weightless, suspended, in a world that was entirely their own; when their hearts had cried out to each other and had been answered. She had in that moment given her heart to Kinnan. But, looking at his strong profile as he steered the boat back into the harbour at Gruz and into sight of *Manta*, she knew with unhappy certainty that it had all been an illusion; and that somehow she must start to live again without it.

CHAPTER FIVE

By the time they were back on board *Manta* Alix had come to terms with her worries. What did it matter if Kinnan didn't love her? she asked herself. *She* loved *him*. She had the warmth of that love to carry through life, even if she never saw him again. Nothing could take that away from her. And it wasn't as if she had ever expected anything different. She had known from the beginning that she was nothing more than a passing irritation to Kinnan, a lame dog to be helped over a stile; nothing, that was, other than an attractive body to be enjoyed and then forgotten.

And now that Vita had arrived, she wasn't even to be that. Kinnan was clearly deeply involved with the sultry journalist, and whatever game they were playing between them had nothing to do with Alix. The engagement Kinnan had sprung on her yesterday hadn't been mentioned again, and Alix didn't wholly believe his excuse that it had been to keep her name out of the gossip columns. Though no doubt Vita would be quick enough to use that method of causing her embarrassment if it would do her own position any good! No, it was more likely that Vita and he had quarrelled before Kinnan left England and she had taken the opportunity to follow him here in the hope of patching it up—only neither of them was yet prepared to go as far as apologising. Hence the travel feature Vita was so busy with, and hence the false engagement. No doubt it would be broken off very quickly when the game had been played long enough.

Yet, paradoxically, Alix felt closer to Kinnan than ever before. The long day in the sunshine with its

80

inevitably relaxing influence had a lot to do with it—
but more important still was the diving. Alix knew that
Kinnan had been pleased and surprised by her
enthusiastic reaction to the underwater world that
obviously meant so much to him. Their conversation
since climbing back aboard the boat had been solely
concerned with that world and the exploration of it,
and Alix, listening and watching, detected an enthusiasm
in Kinnan that had never palled. She guessed that he
still felt, on every dive, the excitement that she had
known on her first timid foray underwater. And she
longed to feel it again herself; to make more and deeper
dives, to learn all that she could about this fascinating
new pastime.

But now the dream was over. They were back on
Manta, back in a world made up of tensions and
conflict. The peace of the tiny island was itself
another world. And as if to emphasise that, Vita
appeared on deck as Kinnan brought the motor-boat
alongside.

'The voyagers return!' Her voice was mocking and
Alix looked up at her. In the fading light, Vita looked
more beautiful than ever in a silky jumpsuit of electric
blue that clung to every line of her richly curving figure.
Long eardrops glittered under her cloud of black hair,
and her eyes shimmered with an eyeshadow that exactly
matched the colour of her clothes. On her feet were
silver sandals, their fragile straps and stiletto heels
making them entirely unsuitable wear for a boat, and
yet she got away with them, just as she would get away
with the most outrageous outfit, Alix thought as she
climbed aboard. Her own shorts and shirt seemed
childish and plain now; but if she tried to dress as Vita
did she would simply look ridiculous.

'Hi, Vita. Had a good day?' Kinnan's voice was
casual and Alix saw Vita shoot a penetrating glance at
him. So the proud beauty wasn't so certain of her lover

as she seemed! There was definitely suspicion in those smouldering eyes.

'I've done very well, thank you. Got all I needed for my travel feature. And you?'

'A great success,' he told her blandly. 'Alix is proving to be an ideal mate.'

And did he have to choose just that word? Alix's cheeks flamed as Vita turned her gaze searchingly on her. She must look the picture of guilt, standing there tousled and sunburnt after her day at sea. But so what? They were supposed to be engaged, weren't they? Almost to her own surprise she lifted her chin and looked Vita straight in the eye. Let her think what she liked! And there *had* been that kiss. . . .

'That's wonderful,' said Vita at last, turning back to Kinnan. 'But I'm sure you'll both be pleased to hear the latest news. After all, it must slow you down, Kinnan, having to work with a complete novice.' And there was more in *that* little sentence than met the ear! 'There was a message earlier, Jon's arriving by this afternoon's flight. He should be arriving any time now. In fact——' she lifted her head as a taxi drew up on the quay '—if I'm not very much mistaken, that looks like him now.' She smiled patronisingly at Alix. 'You'll like Jon. He's about your own age—a nice boy.'

'Jon?' Kinnan was beside them now and as the taxi stopped and a tall, slim figure got out dragging a suitcase and sundry other gear, he jumped ashore. 'Hi, you young scoundrel! Over here! Well, you took your time, didn't you?'

The young man paid the driver and turned to grin. 'Considering I knew nothing about the job until yesterday morning I think I did pretty well!' He came forward into the light and Alix saw a friendly face topped by a thatch of thick fair hair. 'Managed to get a flight from Birmingham. Hope I've brought all the gear I'll need—it cost a mint in excess luggage! Hey, this is nice, isn't it? Didn't think I was going to get the chance of much diving this summer. And are these your two new assistants?' His eyes took in Alix and Vita standing side by side on *Manta*'s deck. 'Looks as though you don't need me after all.'

'Oh, I do, though.' Kinnan's reply was heartfelt and Alix knew a momentary stab of disappointment. Hadn't he said she'd been a good 'mate'? But she couldn't have been as much help as an experienced diver, she reminded herself quickly. And Jon was a photographer too, and that was what Kinnan really needed.

'You know Vita Purvis, don't you?' Kinnan was saying, and Alix saw the new arrival's eyes widen. 'She's just giving a hand where she can and covering a couple of her own stories too. And this is Alix Daley, my fiancée, who's proving to be a very good dogsbody and cook. At least——' his grey eyes turned on her, cool and amused '—I hope she is.'

'Heavens!' Alix's hand flew to her mouth. The evening meal—she'd forgotten all about it. 'Look, I'll go and start the supper straightaway. You'll be staying, Mr——?'

'Redmond.' The blue eyes laughed at her though there was surprise and speculation in them too. 'You didn't even wait for Kinnan to finish the introductions! But you'll call me Jon—no room for Misters and Misses on a boat like *Manta*. And I certainly hope I'll be staying for supper—I imagined I'd be living here!' He turned to Kinnan. 'That's all right, isn't it?'

'Good grief, yes. I need you on the spot, not in some hotel. Luckily we've still got a cabin free, so you won't have to share with Vita or Alix——'

'Shame!'

'—but you'll have to have all your gear in there with you, I'm afraid. I usually like to keep one spare so that we can put all the extra stuff out of the way, but we're full house now. O.K., Alix,' he added without turning his head. 'Do something about supper now, there's a good girl. Something pretty substantial too—you must be as hungry as I am, and if I know anything about air travel Jon won't have seen anything other than plastic food for hours. Now then, Jon. . . .'

His voice was already launched into a description of technicalities as Alix went down through the saloon to the galley. She felt deflated, dismissed; the closeness she had thought she and Kinnan had shared during the latter part of the day seemed to have gone, splintered by Vita's abrasive presence. But she liked Jon; he had an open friendliness that was refreshing after the tensions of the past two days. Perhaps his presence would ease things; she could already hear his boyish laugh ringing out at something Kinnan had said, and she smiled as she began preparations for supper.

Vita did not put in an appearance or offer help in any way. But then Alix had never expected her to.

Jon's coming did ease the tensions that had existed aboard *Manta*, and Alix found herself relaxing for the first time since she had met Kinnan. And although she was still conscious of Vita's smouldering presence, she was saved from the barbs the older girl was so good at delivering; the conversation was frankly monopolised by the two men, and, although Vita looked bored and sulky after a while, Alix was enthralled.

Diving stories took most of their attention and she listened, drinking in every word. Between them they seemed to have dived almost everywhere in the world and their opinions differed as to the best diving grounds, though they were totally in agreement that the Great Barrier Reef off Australia surpassed everything else.

'We're going to include it in the film, of course,' said Kinnan. 'It'll be the high spot. And the Caribbean, and the Galapagos Islands. Jon, have you ever been to——'

They were off again, but this time Alix hardly listened. The Great Barrier Reef! How she would love to dive there, seeing for herself the beauty of the life that teemed around this wonder of the world. She wondered if it might ever be possible. Her heart twisted at the thought of diving there with Kinnan—but she knew that could never happen. But if she joined a diving club when she got back home, learned and practised all she could . . . saved all her money. . . . It would startle Bernie, who had always been the first to launch into something new. But she might even take to the idea herself. And if not—well, Alix would just go alone. She was capable, after all—she was managing well enough in Yugoslavia, wasn't she?

After a while she collected up the dishes and washed them. Again no one offered any help—but why should they? she asked herself wryly. This was what she was here for—what she was being paid for. And at that thought she found herself hesitating about returning to the saloon. Why, after all, should she assume the right to join them? She could only be a drag anyway—the conversation was going well without her, punctuated by sudden bursts of laughter. And she *was* tired after her long day in the open air.

All the same, as she went into her own cabin and began to prepare for bed, she felt depressed, left out and unaccountably lonely.

The two men were already immersed in discussion when Alix set off for the market next morning. With fresh fruit and vegetables so readily available close at hand, there was little point in stocking up except at weekends, and she had quickly learnt how much was needed each day. Ice too could be obtained from a lorry that trundled along the quay early each morning, and she took the special coolbox to fill up with that too.

She had not gone far, however, when she was aware of footsteps behind her, and a moment later her skin was tingling to the touch of Kinnan's fingers.

'Carry the basket, lady?' he enquired lazily, and Alix looked at him doubtfully. He couldn't really have come just for that, he was far too busy with his own plans. But he took the basket from her all the same, his grey eyes dancing.

'You're very attentive all of a sudden,' she remarked, wondering if he could sense how uncomfortable she felt. Particularly when his eyes moved over her in that way, taking in the long brown legs in the brief shorts, the way her T-shirt moulded over her slim but curving figure.

'Well, I have to remember we're engaged,' he answered lightly, and Alix winced. If only they were, she thought miserably, instead of just pretending to be.

'Do we have to go on with that farce?' she asked tightly. 'Now that Vita and Jon are here, you can't need me any more, surely. And my money should be through today—I can pay back anything I owe you for the clothes and go. You can forget all about me. Please— wouldn't that be best?'

He stared at her, eyes narrowed. 'Do you really believe that? That our engagement's a farce?' They were nearly at the market now, their voices almost drowned under the hubbub of chatter and bargaining. 'Is that how you see it?'

'Well, isn't it?' she demanded, her heart beginning to beat rapidly at both his words and the expression in his eyes. 'You said yourself it was a pretence—to keep my name out of the gossip columns. Look,' she went on, stopping to face him, 'can't you see that the more it goes on the worse muddle you'll be in? Vita followed you out here, isn't that enough? Anyone can see it's her you really want, you're just using me as a pawn in the game you're playing with her. Well, I don't *like* being used! And if you hadn't taken my passport I'd have left long ago. I don't even know why you did take it—or why you're keeping it.'

'It's the only way of keeping you, it seems,' he murmured. 'And I took it in the first place because I needed it to comply with the law—the Yugoslavs like to keep track of their visitors, you know. You are now officially on the crew list as cook.' His voice hardened. 'And there's something else you seem to have forgotten—that little score we have to settle. I meant what I said, you know.'

Alix's head snapped up, her eyes wide. Yes, he was a man who would always mean what he said—and get what he wanted, too. Dizzily, she licked her lips and saw his eyes follow the movement. In desperation, she sought to escape—but his hand closed firmly round her wrist.

'Don't try it,' he advised softly. 'There's nowhere to run to, and you'd only make yourself look foolish. Now, shall we get this shopping done? Don't forget, we're both workers, and there's a lot to do.'

'Workers!' she spat at him. '*I* may be, Kinnan Macrae, in fact I most certainly am—but *you*! You've never known a day's real work in your life—it's all pleasure for you, and an opportunity to make even more money without any real effort!'

'I'm warning you,' he gritted, and his fingers tightened painfully on her arm. 'One more crack like that and I'll give you a lesson in manners here and now—and one you won't like at all, although I'm sure it will prove most amusing for the spectators!'

There was no mistaking his meaning, or his capability of carrying out the threat. His free hand was holding the basket, but by the way he moved it she guessed he was itching to apply it with some force to the seat of her shorts. She squirmed with panic and looked up at him imploringly.

'All right,' he grunted. 'I won't—this time. But remember, that was your last warning. I've had just about as much as I can take from you.'

'So why not let me go?' she begged, but he only shook his head.

'I told you, I still need you. Now start earning your keep, little spitfire. Vegetables first. What were you planning to give us for supper tonight?'

She hadn't been planning anything, but with Kinnan by her side, her wrist still held firmly in his iron fingers, she had to start thinking. And rather to her surprise, the exercise helped. The tension between them eased fractionally and by the time they were making their way back to *Manta*, having also been to the bank and collected new travellers' cheques to replace the ones Alix had lost, Kinnan was merely holding her hand—almost, she thought ruefully, as a lover might do. Except that a lover wouldn't be alert for her slightest effort to get away, when the fingers would once more clamp round her arm like a pair of policeman's handcuffs!

Just before they reached *Manta*, Kinnan paused and looked down at her. His eyes were thoughtful.

'Now, what are we going to do with you for the day?' he asked reflectively. 'I'd intended taking you out to the island again, since you seemed to pick up the essentials so well yesterday. But Vita was keen to come, and as she needs a little more local colour for her travel feature I agreed to take her. But I don't want you left roaming about alone—you just might take it into your head to do something foolish. Perhaps you'd better go with Jon.'

'But isn't Jon going with you?' Alix asked. She was conscious of an unreasonable disappointment that he wasn't taking her to the island—together with a stab of pure jealousy that it was Vita who was going instead. And hadn't Kinnan said something yesterday about it not being Vita's scene?

Kinnan shook his head. 'Jon's going into the old city. They've got a very good aquarium there and he's going to have a look at that and a talk with the curator. I'll be going in myself too, of course, but Jon can get a lot of the early stuff dealt with first. Yes, you'd better go with him. You wanted to see the old city anyway.'

Yes, but not with Jon or anyone else, Alix thought rebelliously. I wanted to see it with you! She glanced at Kinnan and had the most uncomfortable feeling that he knew exactly what she was thinking. If only he didn't have such piercing eyes—they seemed to see right into her mind. Turning away, she shrugged and said: 'Suits me. Jon seems a nice person.'

'Oh, he is,' Kinnan agreed gravely. 'And the soul of honour. You have nothing to fear from him.' *Not as you have from me*, his eyes said as they slid over her. Alix felt a faint flush rise to her cheeks as she stepped away from him to go aboard *Manta*, and she bit her lip as she heard his infuriating chuckle.

There seemed to be nothing she could do to alter Kinnan's arrangements, much as she seethed at the way he was ordering her life, and there was no mistaking the light that came into Jon's eyes when he heard that she was to accompany him into Dubrovnik. Nor was there any way of escaping the triumph in Vita's expression when she heard that she was to have Kinnan to herself all day.

'I should be able to take some good photographs,' she said in her husky voice, giving Kinnan a provocative glance. 'After all, they say a picture's worth a thousand words! And we'll have time for a little relaxation, won't we, darling? You won't be working *all* day?'

'I never forget my siesta,' he agreed gravely, his glance flicking over Alix, and her face burned as she remembered the previous afternoon. No doubt Vita would be more compliant than she had been; there would be no inhibitions there about lying in Kinnan's arms on the rocky beach—or about the bathe afterwards. Her imagination conjured up a picture of Kinnan and Vita together in the water, their naked bodies coming together in a flurry of glittering spray. . . . With a sudden abrupt movement, she got up from the table and began to collect up the breakfast dishes.

'Have you been to Dubrovnik before?' she asked Jon politely as they walked along the quay to catch a bus to the old city. She wasn't really interested in his reply; her thoughts were already out in the Inlet with the boat that carried Kinnan and Vita to the island. But that wasn't Jon's fault, and she felt an obligation to make conversation of some sort.

'Came here for a week about three years ago,' he told her as they climbed aboard the bus and he paid the fares. 'I was on one of those package holidays—week here and a week at Split. What you might call a split holiday!'

Alix groaned dutifully. She had already suffered a good many of Jon's puns and realised that he took very few things seriously—on the surface, anyway. But he was pleasant to be with, and clearly more than interested in her.

'I never thought old Kinnan would take the plunge,' he remarked as the bus topped a hill and came within sight of the sea. 'Or is that the wrong expression to use for a diver. . . . But I admire his taste, though it did take me by surprise at first.'

'I suppose you thought Vita was more in his line,' said Alix, guiltily aware that she shouldn't be encouraging Jon to gossip, but unable to resist the opportunity to learn more about her so-called fiancé. 'They certainly seem to be on quite close terms.'

'Mm, you're right. A lot of people did expect——' Jon pulled himself up short with a quick glance at her face. 'Sorry. Not very tactful of me, especially with Vita on the spot. Anyway, you don't have to worry. You've obviously got something she hasn't.'

'Difficult to see what, perhaps,' Alix suggested with a smile to show that she wasn't taking the conversation seriously.

'Now there I think you're wrong,' Jon declared. 'You're a completely—ah, here we are. Told you it would only take a few minutes. This is Pile suburb, and that's the gate into the old city.'

Alix got down from the bus and stood looking around. The road had widened into a large square here, and there were several buses coming and going. There were Atlas and Kompas tourist offices, each with their windows displaying advertisements for tours and concerts. On the opposite side of the road was a large space of ground with several souvenir stalls already doing a brisk trade, and a large open-air café.

But it was the gateway to the old city that dominated the square, catching and holding her attention with its ancient grandeur. It was a huge bastion against invaders; a great, solid tower of white stone that loomed over the wooden bridge suspended over the moat—dry now, she realised as Jon led her across, and laid out as a pleasant garden, gay with flowers, but once presumably filled from the sea that pounded against the old walls only yards away. Awed, she looked up as they passed under the tower and down a flight of steps to go through the second wall. Building such a fortification must have called for considerable expertise.

And then she was still, brought to an abrupt stop in the gateway by the scene that met her eyes as they came through. Straight ahead there was a broad street, alive with people, but entirely free of traffic. It appeared to be paved with marble; the stones shone as if they were wet, and there was a narrow gully running down the centre. To her right a great domed fountain squatted, the water spouting from grotesque images set in its sides. To her left a tall bell-tower rose towards the sky, and this was echoed by another at the extreme end of the street or, as she now remembered it was called, the Placa.

The sun was already brilliant along one side of the Placa, and the shops and cafés were protected by blue awnings. On the shady side the awnings were still furled, ready for the afternoon. The air quivered with the hum of voices; people wandered everywhere, talking, laughing, taking photographs, looking into shop windows, and the whole place vibrated with the atmosphere of holiday.

'Quite a sight, isn't it?' Jon remarked softly. 'I've never been anywhere that quite equals it. As a city, it must be perfect—a medieval gem.'

'It's lovely,' Alix agreed, and once again she wished that Kinnan were here. She had so little to share with him, would have so few memories; she would have liked this to be one of them.

Jon did not appear to be in any great hurry to reach the aquarium and they wandered along the Placa, taking little detours to peer up the narrow side streets, and looking into shop windows. The streets on the left led steeply up to the walls; little more than cracks, Jon told her, when you looked down at them from above.

'You can walk round the entire city on the walls,' he added. 'And it's well worth doing—a real must. Quite a long walk, mind, and too hot during the middle of the day—the white stone increases the heat of the sun—but you get some really spectacular views, especially of the city. All those roofs tumbling crazily about—the city might be built on a grid pattern at ground level but something seems to have happened to it on the way up and it's one glorious muddle up there. If you start at the Pile gateway, you can walk all the way along the landward side to the old harbour, where you have to come down for a short stretch; then you go up again and walk back along the seaward side, with grand views of the cliffs. Altogether, it's quite an experience.'

'Yes, I must do it. I hope I'll get the chance another day,' Alix agreed.

'Oh, you will. Kinnan's based here for a while, isn't he, and he won't let you go away without having seen all there is to see.' Jon gave her a bright, speculative glance. 'That's the old Franciscan monastery over there, by the way—it contains the oldest pharmacy in the world. . . . You know, I was talking to Vita earlier. She hadn't known anything about the engagement either.'

'Nobody did,' said Alix, feeling herself on dangerous ground. Then, something that Jon had said coming back to her: 'Jon—what did you mean when you said something about me having something Vita hadn't got? Can *you* see anything?'

His look was surprised and she wished she hadn't said it. Did it sound as if she was fishing? Or not sure of Kinnan? But it was too late to take it back, and she pretended an interest in some embroidered blouses while Jon pondered.

'Yes, I can,' he said. 'And the long pause wasn't really for thought—I was just considering how to put it. But you've got a nice freshness, a naturalness Vita lost years ago, even if she ever had it. You're straight-forward, direct, honest. I doubt if you'd recognise a subterfuge if it came up and hit you on the nose, let alone use one for your own ends. There's a whole lot more than that too,' he added in a quiet voice, stopping to look into her eyes, 'but unfortunately I don't have the right to say it.'

Alix stared at him, the colour coming into her cheeks. Now she definitely wished she hadn't asked! The last thing she wanted was Jon getting interested in her—just when she'd been looking on him as a kind of no-man's-land, a place where she could be safe from emotion and hurt. For the first time, she was grateful for her pseudo-engagement—at least it would keep him securely at arm's length. Though at one time she wouldn't have

wanted to do so, she thought wistfully. A few days
ago—could it really be only days?—she'd have
welcomed the attentions of someone like Jon. But now
she'd met Kinnan Macrae—and nothing would ever be
the same again. . . .

At the end of the Placa was a large café with a terrace
on the square, its blue awnings gay in the morning
sunshine. Next to it were the columns of the Rector's
Palace where, Jon told her, classical concerts were held
on three evenings each week—'in the Atrium, an
enclosed courtyard,' he explained. 'It's quite an
experience to sit there under the stars listening to
orchestral music. I've never found out what they do
when it rains—but I suppose it doesn't much, during
the summer.'

They went through the café to a second terrace
overlooking the harbour, and sat at a table by the low
wall, under a stone arch, gazing out at the tiny harbour.
Boats danced on the glinting water. The white stone of
the walls led round to another great bastion, the Fort of
St John on the mole; the mole itself, a stone breakwater
extending the harbour's shelter, ran out into the sea,
and Jon told her that people bathed from it.

'There's a nice little pool just round the corner too,'
he added. 'Ideal for diving and swimming—your sort of
diving, not mine,' he added with a grin. 'You might like
to go round there while I'm in the aquarium.'

Alix sipped the iced coffee that she'd ordered. Jon
was drinking *pivo*—Yugoslavian beer—which looked
equally cool and refreshing. They had both refused the
delicious-looking cakes and pastries that had been
offered them—Alix suspected that once you started on
them it might be difficult to stop—but nobody seemed
to mind how long customers sat here. And there was
plenty to look at; boatmen setting off for destinations
such as Lokrum, the island she and Kinnan had seen
yesterday, or Cavtat, a small village down the coast;

small boys fishing in the harbour, young men attending to their boats and flashing their teeth in wide grins at passers-by. And always the tourists, festooned in cameras, their eyes everywhere, their tongues busy with a variety of languages of which Alix recognised only English and German.

'I might do that,' she agreed. 'Just now I'm happy here.' She hesitated, reminding herself once again that gossip wasn't a pleasant thing to indulge in. But there were some things she just had to know. . . . 'Have you known Kinnan long, Jon?'

'Not really. I'm surprised he even knew my name—we've never actually worked together before, though we both work along similar lines. We could almost have ended up as competitors—except that I'm not really in Kinnan's class, and never will be,' he finished with a grin.

'He's really good, then?'

'Oh yes. Top class. But you know that, of course. He ought to be much better known than he is, and he will be before long—this film should see to that—but he's been doing a lot of educational stuff and technical films up to now. Hasn't really gone in for popular filming. But all the ideas are there, and if this new venture comes off——'

'The film, you mean?'

'Well, that's part of it. But I was really thinking of the new TV company. There's been a lot of talk about just what form it'll take and it seems pretty certain that Kinnan will be getting in on the ground floor with the nature spot—which will be a big one. Plus other underwater activities—he's been heavily involved with raising that medieval ship there's all the excitement about, and there are a couple of other finds people haven't heard much about yet. And he's keen on the educational and children's TV too, so it looks as if he's going to have a pretty big finger in the pie. But surely he's told you all this himself?'

'No—not really,' Alix said hastily. 'We—we haven't had much time to talk.' And she blushed furiously as she saw the smile on Jon's face.

'Well, I don't blame you. More important things to discuss, hm? Anyway, it seems that your future husband is all set to become a big TV tycoon, Alix, and once that happens and this film is released—together with a book—the name Kinnan Macrae is going to be a household word.'

So he wouldn't just vanish into the blue, Alix thought. She'd hear about him—see his face even—and be able to follow his progress. And whether that would be a pleasure or a pain, she wasn't just at that moment entirely sure.

'I have to admit,' Jon went on with that disarming grin, 'that I was all the more surprised at finding you engaged to Kinnan—especially with Vita on the spot. I hadn't given her credit for being so bighearted—or maybe Kinnan's so sure of himself that her reaction doesn't matter!'

'I'm sorry?' Alix stared at him, puzzled by his words. They just didn't seem to make sense. 'What do you mean? Why should her reaction matter?'

'Well, surely you must know.' Jon drained his glass, looked into it regretfully and put it back on the table. He started to fish in his pocket. 'Vita's father is Max Purvis. He's a millionaire and he owns the present TV company that's hoping to get the franchise. Kinnan's going in with him—or at least, that's the talk—and everyone assumed that Vita was part of the deal. Including,' he added with a touch of malice in his voice, 'the beautiful Vita herself. *That's* why I was surprised!'

He found some money and called the waiter over to pay the bill. Then he gave Alix a friendly smile and got to his feet.

'You won't mind if I go along to the aquarium now, will you? It's just along there, under the wall. Come along yourself if you like, when you're ready—or go out on to the mole. I'll see you in about an hour if that's O.K., and we'll get some lunch.'

Lunch? She would never want to eat again. And as he disappeared along the harbour and under the wall, Alix sat on at the little table, drinking her iced coffee without even noticing it and staring out at the lively scene with blind eyes.

Now, at last, the reason for her 'engagement' was clear. It was just one step better than an affair— something that Vita's father, his name famous throughout the country, influential in the world of the media and well-known for his strait-laced ideas, would never have countenanced. And it was something that could always be broken off without loss of honour—on either side.

No doubt Kinnan and Vita, alone on the island, were laughing over it even now. No doubt it was only a matter of time before she got her marching orders—and her passport. No doubt the next engagement to be announced would be the one everyone was expecting— to a smiling, triumphant Vita, indulgently forgiving towards her fiancé's temporary lapse.

Until that moment, Alix had never admitted to herself her deeply-felt longing for the charade to turn into truth; her yearning for Kinnan's love, for his voice telling her that he wanted to marry her. But she knew now that it had been there; that it had been in her mind even when she struggled to free herself of him, and that if she had left she would never have been at peace, never have been sure . . . .

Well, she was sure now. Kinnan Macrae wanted to be a household name. And if marriage to Vita Purvis was one of the steps on that ladder, he wasn't going to miss it out. No way.

CHAPTER SIX

IT was already beginning to grow dark when they
returned to *Manta*, the sun setting the horizon ablaze
and turning the sea to a furnace of glowing orange. The
motor-boat and inflatable dinghy were already there,
Alix noticed, nudging the stern of the ketch where they
were moored, and she braced herself to meet Kinnan
and Vita. She could guess just how they would be;
suntanned and blissful after their day alone, their
differences forgotten and their quarrel, whatever it was,
resolved.

Before going aboard, she turned to smile at Jon and
thank him for the day. He had gone out of his way to
make it pleasant for her, she knew; while he was in the
aquarium she had gone back into the city to buy some
food for lunch and explore the market in Gunduliceva
Square. By then, although still busy, it was clearly in its
last stages of the day; she was amused to hear a couple
of English tourists remark disparagingly on how little
there was available, and wanted to point out to them
that the market had been open since at least six o'clock,
when they were probably still in bed. Everything in
Yugoslavia started early; even the banks were open at
seven, and Alix found this exhilarating, for the sun rose
very early indeed and although the clocks ran on
Greenwich Mean Time everything seemed quite
naturally geared two or three hours ahead of English
times.

After a while she had gone to look for Jon in the
aquarium, and finding him still deep in conversation
had spent an hour absorbed in the displays, watching
with fascination as a huge nautilus in its great spiral

shell made its ponderous way across the rocks, while an octopus sent searching tentacles out in all directions. Alix smiled at the starfish but felt sorry for some of the larger fish and the turtles; wouldn't they feel happier roaming free in the limitless oceans? And that thought brought her back to Kinnan and Vita; were they at this moment diving together in the clear waters, sharing the beauty that Kinnan had shown her so short a time ago? If only he had taken her again—but he had obviously had his own reasons for not doing so. And no doubt, she thought, staring unseeingly at a tank full of moray eels, they were good ones; to do with Vita and her father and the forming of a new TV company. . . .

Sadly, she wondered if Vita really loved Kinnan, if she too knew this hunger, this ache of the heart. But Vita had already made it clear that love wasn't necessarily part of her formula for a successful marriage. Material considerations were more important, she'd said, with physical attraction as a bonus. And Kinnan certainly qualified in both those respects.

Maybe he even agreed with her and discounted love from his schemes. After all, if you were ambitious you probably had to. It would only get in the way— especially if it came in the shape of an insignificant little schoolteacher who looked more like a street-urchin anyway. . . .

Jon found her there and guided her out of the darkened aquarium into the brilliant sunshine of the harbour. They took their lunch round the Fort of St John and picked their way along the rocks to a pool, deep enough to dive into yet dazzlingly clear and a mouthwatering aquamarine against the white of the rocks and the soaring walls. There were a few other people there—it was clearly a popular place to come to during the lunch hour for those who worked near enough—but it wasn't crowded, and Alix was as keen as Jon to slip out of her shorts and shirt and dive into the cool water.

The coolness lasted only for a few moments, then the water seemed as warm as a bath. Alix swam and dived, gazing up at the azure sky, thinking how easy it was to float in this densely-salted water and how nice it would be to float here for ever, with no problems or worries. She was just beginning to wonder if she would enjoy being a turtle, or perhaps a dolphin, when Jon surfaced close to her and shook back his hair, grinning. She smiled back at him. He really was rather nice.

'What about some lunch?' he suggested. 'I'm ravenous! And afterwards we'll explore some more of the old city—I want to show you Prijeko. And we'll have an ice at a *slasticarna* I know.'

Prijeko proved to be another street, running parallel with Placa and full of tiny shops and cafés. They spent most of the afternoon browsing along it, looking at embroidered blouses and leather goods, and exploring the tiny alleys that led up to the city walls. Alix was enchanted by their picturesqueness; as the buildings grew taller the upper storeys sprouted ironwork balconies which were a jungle of prolific pot-plants, and washing was festooned from house to house like an array of banners. The scene was full of colour and life; old women in the national dress of black, with a golden flower at the breast, pottered about tending the huge plants or sat at their doors gossiping and sewing, small children darted around their feet and cats sat in impossible positions on the house walls, washing themselves unconcernedly or simply supervising the proceedings with slitted eyes.

Yes, it had been a very pleasant day. The kind of day that one looked forward to and expected while on holiday in a foreign town. They had eaten ices such as she had never seen before and Alix had been unable to resist one of the embroidered blouses and a skirt to go with it. It wasn't Jon's fault that in spite of all this she had felt all the time as if she were only half there, that the colours were somehow dimmed, the sounds muffled. And so as they arrived at *Manta* with the sun burning on the horizon and the stars just beginning to prick through the dark blue velvet of the sky, she turned to smile and thank him as if it had been the most wonderful day of her life.

'It's been grand for me too,' Jon told her quietly. 'Alix—I just want to say——'

But she never heard what he wanted to say. For at that moment there was a sound on deck and Vita appeared, her dark eyes unreadable in the fading light, and surveyed them both with a faint smile.

'Welcome home,' she said, her voice tinged with irony. 'We wondered if you were coming at all, or if you'd decided to make a night of it too.'

'Oh, I'm sorry,' said Alix, immediately washed with guilt. 'It is rather late, isn't it—I'll get on with the meal straightaway.'

'No need.' Kinnan had joined Vita and watched as they came aboard. 'I've decided we'll all go out for our meal tonight. I'm sure you're too tired to start cooking now,' he added to Alix, and she flushed at the edge in his tone.

'No, but it will be nice to go out,' she acknowledged quietly, and wondered what was his reason for this decision. The air was almost electric with tension. Did he think that with four of them together in the boat all evening it could only end in an explosion? She wasn't too sorry herself to be released from the inescapable proximity, and she wondered again how the day had gone between Kinnan and Vita.

She wondered even more when, dressed in the newly-bought embroidered blouse and skirt, she followed the others ashore half an hour later. The two seemed oddly on edge, but it was almost impossible to gauge their

reactions to each other. Vita seemed to alternate
between a violent sulking fit and gay bravado, while
Kinnan had said very little and appeared morose and
short-tempered. Alix couldn't understand it. Just what
had happened out there on the island?

In the short time available she had washed her long
hair and now let it hang loose, drying quickly in the
warm air. The blouse was white with turquoise
embroidery panelling the front and the sleeves; she wore
it over a straight skirt of the same material, catching it
in round her waist with a thin blue corded belt she had
had with her. It was pleasant to feel feminine again,
although she was aware that beside Vita's exotic green
caftan her own outfit was starkly simple and blatantly
touristy—Vita had already guessed just where she had
bought it, and had probably priced it almost to the
dinar. Alix almost wished she had put on her jeans, and
was on the point of doing so when she caught Kinnan's
ironic glance on her and realised that she would only
make herself look all the more ridiculous.

'Don't worry,' Jon muttered in her ear as they walked
along the quay. 'I think you look great, and I should
think Kinnan does too. But he must have told you that
already.'

And just when would he have found a moment? Alix
asked herself bitterly. They hadn't been alone together
for a second since her arrival—Vita had seen to that.
And it didn't seem as if they were going to be now,
either. The little party had already split into two
factions; Kinnan and Vita walking slightly ahead,
laughing and talking in low tones, her hand possessively
on his arm, and Alix and Jon behind, silent, content in
each other's company but acutely aware of the couple
in front.

They went by taxi—no crowded buses for Vita, Alix
noted with a faint inward smile—and got out at the Pile
gateway where the bus had taken them that morning. It

was just as lively in the dark as during the day—even more so, Alix thought with a sudden tiny surge of excitement as she realised that at least one of her dreams was coming true—she was going to experience night-time Dubrovnik with Kinnan, if nothing else. She looked up, finding him at her side, and gave him a happy smile.

'Isn't it lovely? I could roam round Dubrovnik for days, it's so fascinating. Jon says I shall have to walk round the walls before I leave, and I'd like to go to a concert in the Rector's Palace, too. And I saw a notice advertising folk-dancing on the walls, near the harbour—that must be spectacular at night, I wonder if I'll be able to go to that too.' She stopped, aware suddenly that she was chattering, and gave him a cautious sideways glance.

To her dismay his face was dark and sombre. In the shadows she could see finely-drawn lines, making him look suddenly older, and she felt a sudden urge to take him in her arms, draw that tawny head down to her breast and stroke away the harsh lines. But she hadn't the right, she reminded herself miserably. And never would have. It was Vita who would be doing that for him—if she ever felt the need. And she wondered then just how such a marriage would last; a marriage made for convenience, for material reasons, without love. Wouldn't the partners of such a marriage find themselves incredibly, unbearably lonely?

'You obviously enjoyed your day.' His voice was strange, as harsh as the lines on his face.

'Yes, I did,' Alix admitted honestly. 'Jon's very good company and took a lot of trouble to show me things. I wouldn't have enjoyed it half so much on my own.'

Kinnan grunted. It was almost as if he hadn't wanted to hear that—would rather she *hadn't* enjoyed the day. But that was ridiculous, surely? He wouldn't—surely he couldn't hate her as much as that? Even if she had complicated his relationship with Vita and therefore his plans for the future?

Deflated, Alix trudged beside him in silence. Jon and Vita were ahead now, though Vita clearly would rather have been with Kinnan; she kept glancing back over her shoulder, throwing seductive looks at him and ignoring Alix completely. But Jon was holding her arm and Alix guessed that he was deliberately drawing Vita along with him, thinking probably that she and Kinnan ought to be given some time together. We're an engaged couple, after all, she thought, and felt a bubble of hysteria rise in her throat.

'You seem to be amused.' They were passing under the great gateway now, together with a throng of people, and Kinnan stopped for a moment, his fingers holding her elbow so that she was forced to stop too. Jon and Vita disappeared ahead of them and Alix looked nervously at Kinnan. But he couldn't do anything to her with all these people here . . . could he?

'What's the joke?' he persisted. 'Tell me—I could do with a laugh.'

Alix swallowed. 'Nothing,' she managed, her throat dry as she looked up at his face, wondering what could possibly have happened to make him look so morose. Had Vita refused him? And did that mean the end of all his ambitions? But the other girl had seemed so triumphant—as if she was gloating over her victory. Maybe it was just that he was tired of having Alix around, that he wanted to be free of her and able to enjoy himself with Vita, but couldn't. He had to keep up the pretence of the engagement if only for the sake of appearances. And that would be enough to sour any man in love, she guessed. Because she was quite certain that, whatever Vita's own feelings—if she had any at all—Kinnan was quite definitely in love. And, remembering her thoughts earlier about the likely success or otherwise of an arranged marriage, she felt a sudden compassion for him.

'Nothing's funny,' she told him gently. 'At least, nothing important. Shall we catch up with the others, Kinnan? They'll be wondering where we've got to.'

'And that would never do,' he agreed tonelessly. Then, his grey eyes darkening to smoky pewter, he caught her to him. His arms held her with a desperate urgency and his lips were warm and hard as they claimed her own. 'Alix!' he ground out, and then could only groan as their bodies met with a force that made her gasp. The crowds of people swirling round them seemed to fade and disappear; there was nothing in the world but Kinnan's lips on hers, Kinnan's arms holding her close against him. Alix let him mould her body to his, thrilling to the hardness of him. Her worries and fears seemed to disappear; she lifted her face to his, let her hands slide up the rippling muscles of his back, and allowed her lips to respond with an ardour she had never suspected she could feel.

'Hey, break it up, you two! Vita's going mad with hunger down there, and I'm not far off myself!'

They parted reluctantly, with a muttered oath from Kinnan, and Alix stared, dazed, at Jon's grinning face. She felt herself blush scarlet as she realised where she was and what had been happening, and stepped hastily away from Kinnan, looking at him in mortification.

But to her surprise Kinnan didn't seem to be at all taken aback. He merely grinned back at Jon and said easily: 'Well, I haven't seen her all day, you know. And you can tell Vita not to panic—we're eating at that place on the right, just inside the gate.' He slipped his arm around Alix's shoulders. 'Come on, darling. Not all of us can live on kisses, it seems!'

For the first time, Alix blessed the pseudo-engagement; at least it gave an excuse for moments such as this! But she still felt dazed and bewildered as Kinnan led her through the gateway and over to Onofrio's fountain, where Vita was waiting impatiently.

Whatever had got into him? A few moments before he had been terse and bad-tempered. Now he was smiling, fending off Vita's barbed remarks with an urbane nonchalance that had the older girl smouldering. What did it mean?

For one thing, Alix determined, it meant she must make a renewed effort to get away. She didn't regret the kiss at all; it had given her a glimpse of heaven that she would treasure through the lonely years ahead. But she didn't need a course in human psychology to know that if Vita hadn't been an enemy before, she certainly was now. And that could make life very uncomfortable indeed.

The restaurant was an open-air one, right under the city walls, its large courtyard surrounded by a covered terrace. The tables in the courtyard were gay with red tablecloths. In a corner there was a dais where a band played dance music, and in the very centre of the courtyard a space was cleared for dancing.

Kinnan led the way to a table on the terrace and a waiter handed them all menus.

Still dazed, Alix found it difficult to take in what the menu said. In any case, many of the names were Yugoslavian and meant nothing to her—apart from *Raznjici*, which she knew were kebabs, there was nothing she recognised. She looked up ruefully and met Kinnan's glance.

'I'd like fish,' she volunteered. 'Could you choose something for me?' And she handed the menu back.

'You really ought to learn the names of the dishes, you know,' Vita drawled. 'Or how will you manage when you're on your own? Didn't I hear you say something about leaving soon?'

Startled, Alix caught the malice in her voice. *Had* she mentioned leaving in Vita's hearing? She looked again at Kinnan, wondering if he had said anything—if he'd told Vita the whole story—but his expression was unreadable. He called the waiter over, giving his order in fluent Serbo-Croat.

'Marvellous at languages, isn't he?' Vita remarked to Alix. 'Learns them like doing a crossword puzzle—but of course you'd know about that, wouldn't you?'

It was as if she were all too well aware of just how short a time it was since Alix and Kinnan had met, of how very little Alix did know of him, and was losing no opportunity to say so. Alix said nothing, but before Vita could speak again Kinnan said:

'I've ordered a mixed fish platter for us all. Simpler than a lot of different dishes. And a Riesling to go with it, of course.'

Talk about high-handedness! Alix thought. If she hadn't wanted fish herself, she'd have felt very indignant. But neither Jon or Vita seemed to object, and she supposed it was no more high-handed really than her own decisions on food when they ate on the boat. She sat quietly as the others talked, watching other people, listening to the music and looking up at the sky that hung like a dark, sparkling canopy over the courtyard. Over and over again she relived the kiss Kinnan had given her—it seemed a lifetime ago already—and wondered what had prompted it. He seemed as far away now as he ever had, as he leaned back in his chair, taking little part in the conversation himself, watching them with hooded eyes. Alix wondered if it would ever be possible to understand him, if anyone ever had learned the convolutions of his complex personality. She knew so little about him—a fact which Vita had divined with a disconcerting rapidity. Did he have parents, brothers or sisters? Where was his home? Some semi-stately mansion somewhere, no doubt, and his father the local squire. He bore all the marks of wealth; carrying it so casually that he must have grown up with it. Her former revulsion against wealth shook her again; how could she have forgotten it? How could she have let a few kisses, a burning glance or two, drive the memories from her mind—the memories of what too much money could do. . . .

She thought of her own home, the unpretentious house behind the village shop. The pleasure in simple things—a picnic by the sea, a country ramble. The values she had grown up with; the integrity she had seen and admired in her parents and tried to emulate.

Stephen had had the same upbringing, she thought with a pang. But when the crunch had come, it hadn't helped him. Was it something wrong in the values themselves—or was it simply that he was weak and unable to withstand the pressures?

Whatever the reason, he had been as happy as the rest of them until money had ruined him. And so it could, in the same way, ruin anyone who wasn't strong enough to handle it.

She looked at Kinnan, casually elegant tonight in suede slacks and a silk shirt, each in toning shades of pale silver-grey that set off his mane of auburn hair and matched his smoky eyes. The gold at his wrist gleamed dully. Yes, there was money there all right; more money than Stephen had ever had, certainly more than he would have been able to handle.

Kinnan Macrae obviously *could* handle it. But that didn't make it right. It just meant that others—people like Stephen, young and inexperienced and reckless—would try to copy his lifestyle. With results that Alix knew from personal experience could be tragic.

Kinnan glanced up suddenly, caught her gaze and gave her a long, slow smile that turned her heart over. But she wasn't going to be caught any more, she told herself, controlling her own impulses and returning his smile with a level gaze before turning deliberately away. Kinnan Macrae and his like moved in a different world from hers. And that was the way it was going to stay.

The meal was delicious when it came, and Alix had to admit that Kinnan had known what he was doing when he ordered it. How many bottles of Riesling came and went, she never knew, but after a time she began to feel as if she were taking part in a dream. The conversation flowed and she found herself taking an active part in it; laughing, talking, waving her fork to emphasise the points she made. She told stories of her life at school; was aware of Jon's interest, of Vita's sulks and, increasingly, of Kinnan's brooding silence and watchfulness. So what? she thought recklessly, taking some more wine. She'd stayed in the background long enough. It was time she started to enjoy herself, and if Kinnan Macrae didn't like it—well, that was just too bad.

Her head thrown back in laughter at one of Jon's puns, she reached again for the wine bottle—and found her hand arrested, her wrist held firm and immobile in Kinnan's iron fingers.

'Let go!' Alix exclaimed, turning indignant eyes on him.

'When I'm good and ready,' Kinnan retorted, his voice like granite. 'And that won't be while you're still hitting the bottle, Alix my love.'

'Hitting the——' Indignation caught the words in her throat. 'I'm only enjoying myself!'

'That's all too plain,' he remarked drily, and rose to his feet, dragging Alix with him. 'You two stay here and have some coffee and liqueurs—I can recommend the *maraschino*. Or the *slivovika*. Don't hurry, Alix and I are going back to *Manta*.'

'But I don't want to go yet,' Alix protested childishly. 'I told you, I was enjoying myself.'

'And *I* told *you*, you've had enough,' he reminded her curtly, adding under his breath, 'and so have I. Now, are you coming quietly—or do we have a scene?'

'Oh, I should go quietly if I were you,' Vita remarked softly. 'Kinnan just *hates* scenes.'

Alix glanced at her. The other girl was smiling a
catlike smile. She was obviously enjoying every second
of Alix's humiliation, and Alix realised with a flash of
insight that a scene was just what Vita wanted—and
just why she had used that provocative tone. It would
suit her down to the ground to have Alix make a scene,
thus incurring the full weight of Kinnan's wrath.

'No,' she said, controlling her anger with a
superhuman effort, 'I'm not going to make a scene. If
you insist on taking me back to *Manta*, Kinnan, there's
nothing I can do to stop you; after all, you're very
much bigger than I am!'

That squared things a little, she thought, enjoying the
implication that force was Kinnan's only advantage.
She saw his face darken and turned to Jon. 'I'll see you
later, Jon,' she said with a sweet smile. 'And once
again—thank you for giving me such a lovely day.' And
before Kinnan, his hand still round her wrist, could
stop her, she had leant forward and given Jon a kiss full
on the mouth.

Maybe it wasn't fair, she thought a little repentantly
as Kinnan led her across the courtyard, his fingers
biting cruelly into the soft flesh of her wrist. But it had
been worth it, just to see the looks on their faces!

Kinnan did not speak a word as they found a taxi
and drove the short distance back to Gruz. His face in
the dim light that filtered through the windows was set
and expressionless, but a small muscle twitched in his
cheek and Alix knew that he was angry. She trembled a
little; was he going to take the opportunity now to teach
her that lesson he'd promised her? But what had she
done to make him so angry? What had she said?

The taxi drew up on the quay and they got out.
Kinnan paid the driver and then marched her across to
Manta. As if I'd try to run away now, she thought
rebelliously. Where could I go at this time of night? But
she knew that if he did let go, sheer panic might make

her run, and her destination would be in the lap of the gods.

They climbed aboard and Kinnan gave her a little push towards the saloon. Submissively, her heart thudding with fear, Alix went down the steps and sat down on one of the berths.

Kinnan switched on the light and sat down opposite her.

'Now then,' he said, and his voice was quiet, silky and infinitely menacing, 'maybe you'd like to explain to me just what it is you're playing at?'

'Playing at?' Alix repeated, her voice quavering. 'I don't know what you mean.'

'And don't give me that,' he snarled. 'You've been blowing hot and cold all evening—kissing me like that in the gateway——'

'You kissed *me!'*

'Don't say you didn't co-operate,' he retorted. 'You enjoyed it as much as I did—you *wanted* it as much as I did. And then, in the restaurant, you just gave me the cold shoulder—behaved as if I wasn't there. What is it? What's got into you?'

'Nothing!' She gazed at him helplessly. How could she explain? He would never understand her feelings about money, never see that this was an insurmountable barrier between them. She sought some explanation that he could understand and accept, even if it were not the real one. 'Yes, all right, I enjoyed the kiss. But that's all it was—a kiss. It didn't mean anything. It couldn't. You've got Vita and I——'

'Oh yes,' he said slowly, staring at her as if he had never really seen her before. 'You've got Bernie, haven't you? But Bernie's not here.' With a quick, lithe movement he was beside her, his hands on her arms. 'And neither is Vita, just at the moment. And I did promise to—educate you a little, didn't I? I shouldn't imagine you think you've much to learn—but there may be one or two things that even Bernie hasn't been able to teach you. . . .' His lips came nearer and Alix watched in fascinated horror, her own parting as she struggled to protest. And then his mouth was on hers, his hand was covering her breast and already her struggles were weakened by the surge of longing and desire that swept her from head to toe. Feebly, she tried to push him away, but his chest was like a rock against her hands and almost to her surprise she found her fingers fumbling instead with the buttons of his shirt, probing inside to find the warm flesh and the strong, steady heartbeat.

'You've driven me mad long enough, Alix,' he muttered against her lips. 'I've tried everything I know to keep you here, but every time I turn my back I'm afraid you'll run away. Maybe this will persuade you— but if it doesn't, at least we'll have known what we're throwing away!'

Alix scarcely understood his words; she was aware only of his hands sliding up her body, slipping the blouse over her head, moving sensuously on her bare skin as he removed her bra. She moved languorously in his arms, seeking his skin with her lips, and shivered as he cupped his hands over her breasts, gently pinching the nipples between his fingertips, and bent his head to nip them in his teeth.

'Alix,' he muttered, so low that she barely heard him. 'Alix, you're not to go away. Don't you understand, Alix—I love you. I think I've loved you from the moment I saw you there in Kotor, so lost and alone. I swore I'd go back and find you—but I didn't have to, did I? You came to me. Alix . . . Alix. . . .'

Delight soared through her body, lifting her it seemed to some mountain peak far removed from the ordinary everyday world, raising them both to a pinnacle of love. Alix ran her fingers through his hair and down his back. He loved her! Kinnan loved her—and now, at last, she could acknowledge her own love for him. She murmured his name and he raised his head to look at her. His eyes were dark, almost black, and she trembled at their expression.

'I love you too, Kinnan,' she breathed, and felt the blood pulse through her veins, quickening her heartbeat. Reaching up, she let her fingers tangle in the coppery hair and drew his face down to hers, closing her eyes as his lips touched her brows, her cheeks, her ears and her throat. Restlessly, she moved under him, wanting the abrasion of his skin against hers, and twined her legs around his. Somewhere, in a tiny detached corner of her mind, she was amazed at her own behaviour—she'd never gone as far as this before, had thought herself too inhibited. But now . . . she looked into Kinnan's eyes as he murmured again of love. And knew that before they went any further she must clear up at least one misunderstanding.

'Kinnan,' she whispered, knowing that at this moment there must be nothing but truth between them. 'Kinnan, I've got to tell you——'

He laid his finger on her lips. 'No confessions now, my love. This is our moment—nobody else's.'

'But I must!' She shifted in his arms. 'It's about Bernie——'

His expression darkened. 'Alix, do you have to?'

'Yes. You see—you don't know the truth about Bernie. I—I let you think Bernie was my boy-friend, but that's not true. I——'

Kinnan stiffened and drew himself away. His face was suspicious. 'Alix, are you telling me Bernie's your *husband*? That you're married?'

'*No!* Nothing like that. She—Bernie's a *girl*, Kinnan. I—I've never had a serious boy-friend. I—I'm a virgin.'

There was a silence. Alix peeped up at him uncertainly. Was he angry? But why? She'd had to tell him.

'Are you telling me the truth now, Alix?' he asked at last, and she nodded.

'There was never anyone—I never wanted to——' she stammered, and he nodded almost absently.

'So you've never made love before.'

She shook her head and reached for him. 'But I'm ready now, Kinnan,' she whispered. 'Love me now—please!'

He looked down at her and she saw with a sinking heart that he was beginning to button his shirt again. Suddenly frantic, she sat up, pressing herself against him, moving her swollen breasts against his chest, but he shook his head and pushed her gently away.

'Don't do that, Alix,' he said in a low voice. 'It won't work. I can't make love to you now—like this. We've got to talk things out. We've got to see where we go from here—if anywhere. We've got to be sure.'

'But I *am* sure! I love you. I want you—I thought you wanted me!'

'My God, do you think I don't now?' he burst out, flinging himself away from her. 'I told you, you've been driving me wild! I was prepared to do anything to make you realise—I *had* to love you, even if it was only once, just to get you out of my system. There isn't *room* for you in my life, can't you see that—but I knew I'd never rest easy till I'd at least finished what we'd started. But now—everything's different. I don't go around seducing virgins, Alix. That's a totally different thing from having an affair with a girl who's experienced and knows what it's all about. I don't pretend I haven't done that in my time—or that I wasn't prepared to do it again. But now that I know—I just *can't*!'

Alix stared at him, her hazel eyes wide in her pale face. She listened to everything he said, but only one sentence remained in her mind. *There's no room in my life for you.* No room. The words pealed through her consciousness like the bells of doom. There was no room in Kinnan's life for her; he'd never intended any permanent relationship; she was just a passing experience, something to be got out of his system. Like a disease.

'Then maybe you'd better let me go after all,' she said in a tight voice. 'I seem to be wrecking your whole career while you keep me here. And then you'll be able to get on with your plans, won't you? I'm sure Vita is only waiting for you to say the word.'

Kinnan looked at her. His face was drawn and haggard by his emotions, and when he spoke his voice was dry and husky.

'Get into your cabin,' he said thickly. 'Get in there and stay there. And take my advice and bolt the door— I just don't feel responsible for my actions tonight, and I don't want anything to happen that we'll both regret later.'

Without a word, although her legs were shaking, Alix got up and moved across the cabin. She did not look at Kinnan again as she opened her own door; but as she closed it she caught a glimpse of him sitting there, his head buried in his hands as he leaned on the table.

She closed the door and bolted it. She didn't know if Kinnan had meant it, if he really would come to her in the night. But she did know that if he did she just wouldn't be able to cope any more. And she agreed with him in that they didn't want to have anything to regret later.

Not that she was sure she didn't already have plenty to regret. And meeting Kinnan Macrae, she thought unhappily, was probably the most regrettable thing that had ever happened to her.

CHAPTER SEVEN

ALIX did not get up early the next morning to go to the
market. After a restless night, with what sleep she did
get disturbed by dreams figuring Kinnan wearing a
wetsuit and fins while she floundered helpless and
drowning just out of his reach, she fell into a heavy
slumber just before dawn broke, and remained dead to
the world until after eight o'clock.

She was finally woken by a violent hammering on the
door. Startled and shaken, not at all sure of where she
was, she jerked upright and stared around the cabin.
And then memory flooded back and she lay down
again, pulling the blankets over her ears, wishing
miserably that she could shut out the whole of the past
week, go back and start again.

'Return to Go,' she muttered half hysterically. 'Do
not collect two hundred pounds . . . oh, who *is* that?'

'Alix!' Kinnan's voice shouted angrily. '*Alix*, are you
going to answer or shall I break down this door?'

'It's your boat,' she retorted. 'Look, won't you wait a
minute, I've only just woken up.'

'No, I can't. I want to see you, and I want to see you
this minute!' The hammering increased.

Wearily, feeling sick and dazed with sleep, Alix
swung her legs off the bunk and reached across the tiny
cabin to open the door. She brushed her hair back from
her face and looked up.

Kinnan was standing there clad only in brief denim
shorts, and even at that moment she couldn't help
noticing just how handsome he was; how rugged his
body, hard and firm with the muscles that rippled their
way from ankle to shoulder; how tanned he was; how

116

attractive the face that looked down at her, with finely-chiselled mouth, silver-grey eyes and red-brown hair. Even though he was so drawn and haggard . . . as if he too had spent a sleepless night. . . .

'Well?' she muttered, glancing away. She couldn't afford to let him get beneath her guard now, and as she saw his glance travel over her she hastily pulled together the front of her flimsy nightdress and drew the sheet over her body.

'I just wanted to make sure you were all right,' he said harshly. 'It's after eight, you know. Or maybe you were intending to spend the day in bed—recovering?'

'I've nothing to recover from——' she began indignantly, and winced as a sharp pain jerked through her head. 'Anyway, there's food aboard for tonight—the stuff I got yesterday. I presume you've already decided who's to prepare it, since I shan't be here.'

'Oh, don't talk so silly, Alix,' he said wearily. 'You know you're not ready to go on—you know you don't want to go at all really——'

'I know nothing of the kind! And will you please stop telling me what I know—or what you think I know? I *do* want to go—I've been telling you for days—I never wanted to stay in the first place, and now I've got my money——'

'Oh yes, money,' he cut in. 'That's the important thing, isn't it? I take it you've drawn up an invoice for me? With different rates for the time you've spent as cook, washer-up, shopper? And we mustn't forget the assistance you gave me during my diving, of course. I wouldn't dream of not paying the going rate for that—all of it. . . .'

Her hand cracked across his cheek almost before she realised it, and then she backed away, remembering the last time she had slapped him and terrified of what he might do to her now. But as she crouched there on the bed, staring up at him with wide eyes, all too aware that this time there was no escape, he remained motionless, watching her with eyes that had turned to granite. She could see a pulse beating strongly under the brown skin of his neck; saw his eyes widen and then narrow to slits; saw his fingers curl and then uncurl, the movement running up the tendons of his arms. And she felt the tension increase until it must surely be at breaking-point.

And then, just as she knew that she could hold her breath no longer, he moved. Alix felt herself shrivel under the iciness of his gaze, before he moved abruptly, out of the cabin, without another word, and left her there in silence, staring at the closed door.

He hadn't just closed the door to her cabin, she realised dully, he'd closed the door to his mind. And to his heart.

How long she sat there, she never really knew. She heard movements, voices; the sound of the little motor-boat starting up and chugging away across the harbour; silence except for the normal sounds of rigging slapping against masts, the friendly voices of other yachtsmen, the calls of the stallholders on the quay. But none of these seemed a part of Alix's world. They seemed to be something alien, like watching a film, knowing that the characters whose story seemed so important were in fact mere images whose tragedies and dilemmas could be forgotten as soon as the credits rolled up the screen. They were there, but she was alone and whether she stayed or went meant nothing to them.

At last she got slowly off the bunk and washed in the shower-room. She took a long time over it, but felt no different when she had finished. She was still numb with a pain she hadn't yet started to feel.

Breakfast was beyond her, apart from a glass of orange juice. But she forced herself to pack, meth-odically filling her new rucksack with the clothes she had bought. They would offset anything she might be said to have earned; she didn't feel inclined to argue about it. All she needed now was her passport, which Kinnan presumably kept in his cabin. She would find that after she had taken her rucksack on deck.

She ducked up through the hatchway, dragging the rucksack after her—and stopped dead.

Vita was lying on the deck, wearing a scarlet bikini. She had a book in front of her, but she didn't seem to be reading it; in fact, to Alix it seemed as if she had been watching the hatch, waiting for her appearance. Her face was sleepy and smiling, but her eyes were watchful.

'Going somewhere?' she enquired, her voice silky. 'I thought I heard you say something to Kinnan about leaving, but I couldn't really believe it. Although after last night. . . .' She left the sentence unfinished, but it wasn't hard for Alix to complete it. *After last night you could hardly expect to stay, could you?* And her cheeks burned as she recalled last night in every detail—and wondered just how much Vita knew or guessed, and how much she'd heard this morning.

'So you're leaving?' Vita went on. 'Well, we'll miss you, Alix, but it was never really on, you know. That engagement to Kinnan, I mean. Oh, I can understand the way your mind worked—after all, it must have seemed a tremendous opportunity for a little school-teacher, to marry the great Kinnan Macrae. Because that's what he's going to be, you know. He's well-known enough now, but he's going to hit the top before long. Everyone agrees about that.' She smiled and stretched like a cat, showing off her richly curving figure. 'Yes, I can quite see you being swept off your feet, believing him, thinking that it was for real. Poor little thing,' she added indulgently as if Alix were a stray kitten, 'how could you know?'

'Know what?' Alix's mouth was dry, her face stiff. She wanted to look away from Vita but couldn't move her eyes; they remained fixed on the sensuous figure, taking in every detail of voluptuous curves and rich dark hair.

'Why, about Kinnan, of course! He really is a very naughty boy at times,' Vita said confidingly. 'But you can't be angry with him, he really believes in it himself for a time. I had an idea there'd be trouble in Yugoslavia—that's why I came out. And just in time too, it seemed!' She laughed, a bell-like sound that seemed to freeze the blood in Alix's veins. 'It always happens when he's on his own. Some innocent young girl comes along, they get involved in some way or other and before they know where they are they're in love. Or they think they are. It's never genuine, of course—though it may be on the girl's side. That's the tragic part about it.'

'And on Kinnan's?' The words had to be forced out, but she had to ask.

'Oh, as I said, he *believes* it. But it never lasts more than a few days. And then it's all over and——' she stretched again, complacently '—he comes back to me.'

Alix turned away. The revelation was no more than she should have expected, she scolded herself. But somehow she felt more hurt now than by anything Kinnan himself had said or done. To know that it was just one more in a long history of similar events . . . that she was just one in a line of girls. . . . She was leaving, she had made up her mind that she could never be part of Kinnan's life—but she would still have liked to be something special to him, someone he'd remember. From what Vita said, he probably wouldn't even remember her name.

'Don't let me keep you,' she heard the older girl say insinuatingly. 'After all, you must be wanting to get on. Or maybe there's something I can help you with?'

'My passport,' Alix muttered. 'Kinnan kept my passport—I don't know where it is.'

'Oh, that's easy.' Vita swung easily to her feet.' It'll be in his cabin. I'll fetch it for you—I know where he keeps things.' She slipped down into the saloon and went through to Kinnan's cabin while her words struck a fresh arrow into Alix's heart. How could she have let herself love him, she wondered unhappily, when it was so obvious that Vita was the woman he cared for—or at least intended to make his life with. She watched as Vita came back, tossing back her long, raven's-wing hair and smiling.

'Here it is, all safe and sound.' She held it out. 'Now there's nothing to stop you going wherever you like.' So long as it's away from here—the words hung in the air as Alix took the passport.

It should have given her a feeling of freedom, of release. But it didn't; she felt more trapped than ever as she stared down at it. Then she looked up at Vita.

'I heard that Kinnan's going into partnership with your father,' she said dully. 'Will you give him my best wishes, if it comes off? I hope——'

'Oh, it'll come off.' Vita stood there, superbly confident, 'Kinnan knows which side his bread's buttered. Well, you know that—he'd never have made up that engagement if he hadn't been worried about my father, would he?' She moved closer and Alix caught a whiff of exotic perfume as the journalist laid a long, red-nailed finger on her shoulder. 'Just one word of advice, little schoolteacher. Don't try to get in touch with Kinnan again, or start up this—relationship—after this, will you? I could just turn quite nasty if things went wrong between Kinnan and me. And I don't think you'd like to feature in any kind of newspaper story, would you? Sheer entertainment for the masses, of course, but I've heard it can cause quite a lot of trouble in family circles.'

As a threat, it wasn't even veiled. Get out or I'll start a smear campaign. Vita might as well have put it that crudely. Alix stared at her, feeling disgust and nausea, together with a deep compassion for Kinnan if he ever did marry this girl.

But she had to take it seriously. There was no hope of her ever meeting Kinnan again once she'd left—she wasn't even to try. And if the impossible happened and *he* contacted *her*. . . .

Unable to tolerate sharing the same airspace with Vita any more, she stepped quickly away and heaved her rucksack on to her shoulder.

'You needn't worry,' she said bitterly. 'I won't come anywhere near Kinnan again—especially if you're around.'

'Just leave me out of it,' Vita warned. 'Just keep away. Or I'll pull out all the stops.'

Alix nodded, not trusting herself to speak again. Then she turned, jumped ashore and walked quickly away.

At the end of the quay she looked back, her eyes lingering on the graceful sweep of the ketch on which she seemed to have lived through a lifetime of traumatic experience. It was only a few days, yet she seemed to be a different person; an older and sadder person.

But wiser? She doubted it, somehow. Because even now she knew that if Kinnan Macrae were to appear before her, look into her eyes with that heart-turning tenderness in his and take her in his arms, she would be lost. Whatever Vita Purvis, with all her contacts and jealousies and advantages, might threaten.

As she wandered away from the harbour and its tossing boats Alix realised that she had no idea at all as to where she was going or what she was going to do. Her whole idea had been to get away; encouraged by Vita, she had had no time to make plans. She found herself at the bus station, but was disinclined to join the milling throng and get on a bus; besides, there was nowhere she particularly wanted to go. As she hesitated she realised that she still hadn't seen much of Dubrovnik itself. Was there any reason why she shouldn't stay here for a day or two? Kinnan was busy with his diving and writing; neither he nor Jon were likely to go into the old city, and if Vita happened to see her she wasn't likely to draw anyone else's attention to the fact that she was still here.

Slightly cheered by at least having made a decision, Alix walked past the bus station and made her way across the neck of the peninsula towards the coast, following the route the bus had taken when Jon had taken her to the old city. She walked slowly, stopping to peer over cliffs that fell away sheer from the pavement to the sea boiling on the rocks far below. Then she continued on down through Pile, past the hospital and so to the square where the figure of St Blaise, patron saint of Dubrovnik, looked calmly out from his position on the gateway tower as he had done for centuries.

I suppose you've seen it all, she thought, staring up at him. All the battles and the conquests, all the great tragedies and victories as well as the small, personal ones. You've seen them all—maybe you know the answers. Or maybe there just aren't any answers. . . .

It occurred to her that she ought to make some arrangements about the night; she could get rid of her rucksack then and be free of the burden that weighed rather heavily on her shoulders. She remembered that a short way back up the road she had noticed a house advertising rooms, and she turned to go back.

And walked straight into Jon.

'Well, this is an unexpected pleasure,' he said, smiling. 'I thought I was going to have to spend today all alone. But where are you going? You surely haven't seen enough of Dubrovnik?'

Alix shook her head. What was she to tell him? Already he was looking curiously at her rucksack, and

she knew that she had to tell him the truth. 'But you
mustn't tell Kinnan you've seen me,' she added
urgently. 'I'd rather he thought I was a long way
away—and that you didn't know where.'

Jon stared at her. 'You've left *Manta*? And Kinnan?
But why? Surely not because of last night? Oh, I know
he was a bit overbearing, but you don't want to take
any notice of that, Alix. He's been used to having his
own way, that's all—you'd soon adapt to each other.
And he thinks the world of you, you know that.'

'That's just what I don't know,' Alix said bitterly.
'No, Jon, the whole thing was one ghastly mistake. I
should never have let any of it happen. And now——'
she shrugged a little hopelessly '—the best thing for me
to do is get away and forget all about it. But I did want
to see Dubrovnik properly before I left.'

'Hmm.' Jon looked thoughtfully at her. 'So where
were you off to, then? You're heading away from the
city.'

'Yes, I wanted to fix a room—there are some houses
up the road with boards out. I can leave my things there
then.'

'I see. And how long do you mean to stay?'

Alix glanced at him. Clearly he didn't believe her
story. He probably thought that she was hoping
Kinnan would come after her—even that she wanted
him to let Kinnan know where she was, in spite of what
she'd said. She sighed.

'I'm not playing games,' she warned him. 'I mean
what I say. I *don't* want Kinnan to find me—it really is
all over.' She hesitated. 'There's more than you know to
all this, Jon, and I can't tell you the whole story. But
take it from me, Kinnan won't even want to come and
find me once he finds I'm gone. He'll be angry, I expect,
but that's just pride. So please—you won't tell him, will
you?'

'Not if that's what you really want,' Jon agreed,

though she could see he was still doubtful. 'Now, what about this room?' He began to walk up the road beside her.

'But aren't you busy?' Alix asked. She still wasn't sure whether she could trust him; perhaps it would be better if he didn't know exactly where she was staying. 'You must have been going into Dubrovnik for some reason.'

'Mm. Got another appointment at the aquarium. But I've plenty of time for that. And I'll probably be able to help you. Not many people speak English, and didn't you say you didn't know much German?'

'Yes, I only know a few words,' she confessed, realising the difficulties of communicating and feeling grateful for his forethought.

'Well, most people do know German, so I can help you there. I wish I could speak some Serbo-Croat. But I haven't got Kinnan's head for languages.'

'Vita mentioned that,' Alix remarked, feeling a twinge of dislike just at the mention of the other girl's name. 'Is he really good at them?'

'Oh yes—he picks up a new language in no time at all. He says there's a trick to it, once you've learned three or four it suddenly becomes easy. Trouble is learning the first three or four!'

'I only know French,' said Alix, 'and I'm not very good at that. In fact, I'm not all that good at anything!'

'And that's just not true,' Jon said warmly. 'You mustn't disparage yourself, Alix. People take you at your own valuation, you know—and if you keep telling them what a fool you are they'll start to believe you.'

Alix smiled, a little ruefully. Kinnan hadn't needed telling, she thought. He'd known from the beginning that she was scatterbrained and liable to do silly things. They would never have met if she hadn't been. And she still wasn't sure if she wished that they hadn't. She'd known more pain in the past few days than she'd ever believed possible—and she'd known more ecstasy too.

They found a house advertising rooms to let and arranged with the plump, smiling housewife that Alix should have a room for tonight at least and possibly longer. She was thankful for Jon's help; the woman knew no English at all. German was clearly the most useful language to know in Yugoslavia, and Alix determined to learn it before her next visit.

'Right, that's settled,' said Jon as they came out again into the bright sunshine. 'And now what? A walk round the walls?'

'That's what I was thinking of, yes.'

'Good idea. But don't get roasted up there—it's a real suntrap. And when you come down, by the harbour, let's meet for lunch. You'll be ready for some by then.'

Alix hesitated. Did she really want to see Jon again? Could she really be free of *Manta*, and therefore Kinnan, as long as she continued to meet the photographer? But she looked up at Jon's open, friendly face, full now of concern for her and knew that she couldn't refuse. It would be churlish—and he *had* just helped her over the room.

'Yes, I'd like that,' she said with a smile. 'I'll see you there, then. At about one?'

That would give her plenty of time to explore most of the old city. And if she spent the afternoon in seeing the rest, she could leave tomorrow morning. And then there would be nothing to remind her.

It was almost possible, she reflected as she leaned over the white stone wall and looked down at the street far below, to forget Kinnan. For minutes at a time she could manage to put him out of her mind; but each time she did so he would return with renewed force, pushing his way back as if determined to be a part of her. She would see his face, strong and stern yet ready,

with his firm lips and quirking eyebrows, to break into
that smile that she found so devastating. She could feel
the glance of his ice-grey eyes, reflecting the shimmering
colour of the sea before dawn; she shivered at the vivid
memory of his hands on her body, his mouth claiming
hers.

It would be a long time before she had him entirely
out of her system. But she had to try. And she took a
deep breath and continued her walk round the city
walls.

They certainly were spectacular. From the Pile
gateway she had climbed several flights of steps,
spending some time staring with pleasure at the view of
the Placa and hesitating before deciding to follow Jon's
advice and take the inland side first. Then she had
climbed again, to the huge round tower of Minceta,
which her guide book told her had been built during the
fifteenth century. She climbed to the top and stood
looking out over the tiny city that lay at her feet and
beyond it to the shining Adriatic. From here she could
look down the outer side of the walls, seeing how they
appeared to grow from the rocks and soil beneath,
almost like a natural feature. Could they ever have
looked new and garish, or had they looked right from
the moment they were built? The people of the city
must have been awed and proud of their magnificent
construction; they must have felt secure within the new
walls, certain of keeping their precious freedom, for
who could storm such bastions?

If only her heart could be similarly protected! If only
she could erect such walls to keep Kinnan out, to save
her from the pain that was eating at her even now.

But it was too late to put up barriers, even flimsy
ones. That should have been done when she first saw
him, first caught the glance of those silvery eyes that
seemed to pierce right into her mind, first saw the quirk
of the dark eyebrows. When she felt the first touch of

his lips on hers and knew that this man spelt danger, that she should get away, far away, as fast as she could.

She hadn't erected any barriers then. And now it was too late.

'And did you enjoy the walls?'

'Oh, yes!' She couldn't have failed to, she thought as she smiled into Jon's face. All those tumbled red roofs; the tiny cracks between the houses which were their only access; the steep flights of steps leading up from the hollow where the Placa lay to the rim of the bowl on which the walls were built. How did they get furniture up to those houses? she wondered. How did those old women manage their shopping? What about prams? But although her questions remained largely unanswered, none of the people she had looked down on seemed worried about the inaccessibility of their homes. Grandmothers sat outside, knitting or sewing; young wives bustled about with brooms and buckets; children played—at least there was no risk from traffic. And the pot-plants burgeoned everywhere, huge Swiss-cheese plants, flowering bougainvillea, clematis. The city seemed ablaze with flowers.

Jon was watching her. Did he see through her enthusiasm to the unhappiness that lay like a stone in her heart? Alix's flow of words faltered and she stopped talking and picked up the menu.

'I don't really want much to eat, Jon. Just an iced coffee will do, it's too hot to be hungry.'

'And what did you have for breakfast?' he asked.

Alix thought. 'Can't remember.' She recalled the scenes with Kinnan and Vita. 'I don't think I had anything, actually.'

'As I thought.' He turned to the waiter. 'An iced coffee, a *pivo* and two omelettes, please.'

Alix started to protest and then fell silent. She supposed Jon was right, she probably did need something. She looked out across the harbour at the dancing boats. It was all so beautiful, so happy. Yet she felt as if she were miles away; only half of her here, the most important half, the feeling, thinking, loving half somewhere else. Anchored in a small boat, she thought with a sudden contraction of her heart; watching a swimmer far below in the clear, warm water . . .

'Alix,' said Jon when the omelettes had arrived, 'look, I know this isn't the right time to say this to you, but I've got to. You're like a wild bird—you'll fly away if I don't do something to stop you. I might never see you again. So I have to say it now.'

'It's no good,' she said in a trembling voice. 'I can't go back to Kinnan. It's over, Jon, I told you.'

He shook his head. 'I'm not talking about that. Hell, Alix, can't you see—I don't know what there was between you and Kinnan, I don't know what went wrong. But if you really mean what you say—if you really mean it's all over—you're going to need a friend. Someone to turn to, a shoulder to cry on. Someone who won't ask questions.' He reached across the table and took her hand. 'I'm just asking to be your friend, Alix.'

Startled, Alix met his eyes. Blue and ingenuous, they were full of concern—but there was something else lurking behind that concern, a tenderness she couldn't mistake. And she knew that Jon's friendship would go deep into love if given the chance.

The thought was a new one and she considered it with some dismay. Was Jon in love with her—or did he just imagine he was? Or was he perhaps still unaware of it, still thinking of her as Kinnan's, offering friendship out of genuine concern without realising that it could become love? Whichever it was, he was liable to get hurt, and Alix didn't want to hurt him that way.

'Jon——' she began, but he interrupted her, his hand closing firmly on hers.

'You don't have to say it, Alix, I know what I'm doing. I know the score. But ever since I first saw you aboard *Manta* in your shorts and shirt, all windblown and sunburnt, I knew that I'd found what I'd been looking for—a girl who was as fresh and natural as spa water. There's nothing artificial about you, Alix, you're absolutely yourself, and that's what I like. I thought Kinnan liked it too—in fact I'm sure he does—but something's gone wrong between you, and only the two of you know what. Well, I'm not trying to muscle in before the dust settles, but I want you to know this: I'm here and I'll wait, for as long as you like. I'm not going to pressurise you, Alix—but I can't let you go without telling you what's in my mind.' His voice lowered. 'I love you, Alix. We could have a good life together. Just as soon as you're ready.'

Alix's soft hazel eyes brimmed with tears. She stared down at their fingers, intertwined on the check tablecloth, utterly speechless. She knew Jon well enough to realise that this was no casual declaration; he was no womaniser—like Kinnan was, a spiteful inner voice, disconcertingly like Vita's, taunted her—and the love that he offered was genuine and true. It could be nothing else. But could she accept it, feeling the way she did? Could she forget Kinnan, put him firmly in the past, and step forward into a future with Jon? There was no doubt about it—the love she would receive wouldn't be second-best. But the love she gave—could that be anything else?

She raised her eyes and found him watching her anxiously.

'Jon, I don't know what to say——'

'Don't say anything, then,' he cut in gently. 'I know I can't expect any kind of an answer now—except no. And since you haven't given me that—well, at least I can hope. And we will be friends meanwhile, won't we? We'll keep in touch?'

Alix nodded, then said with a shaky laugh: 'You haven't eaten your omelette.'

'Neither have you,' he said. 'Come on, I'll race you. And then we'll have another drink. Are you going to finish your walk round the walls?'

'Yes, I suppose so.'

'I wish I could come with you,' he said, 'but I've got to get back. Kinnan wants to get on with some more preparation and I *am* here to work.'

'And you won't—you won't tell him you saw me?' Alix asked, her mouth suddenly dry.

He shook his head. 'I promised. Trust me, Alix—my love.'

If only Kinnan had spoken to her like that, she thought with a sudden ache in her heart. If only he could have been the one to have fallen in love with her—instead of merely wanting her. How different everything would have been.

But it was no use wishing. Kinnan didn't love her—he never had. He'd felt sorry for her, helped her, and then, when Vita had surprised them in the cabin, he'd covered up his lust by pretending to an engagement that could never have come true. And then he'd had to keep her there to give credence to his lie. Their positions had been reversed—*he* needed *her* because he dared not alienate Vita. He was balancing Alix against his whole future.

It was her misfortune that she had fallen in love with him. Her misfortune that a day off a tiny, deserted island, swimming and diving, should have opened her heart and left her defenceless.

'I must go soon,' said Jon, bringing her back sharply to the present. 'When will I see you again?'

Alix shook her head. 'I don't know. I must have time——'

He nodded. 'I won't press you. But you won't go without letting me know, will you?'

'No, I won't.' She made an effort and smiled at him.

'What about tomorrow evening—here? I'll probably be a bit more human then!'

'You're human now,' said Jon with a smile, and he leaned forward and kissed the tip of her nose. 'Dear Alix! You don't know just how dear you are. Till tomorrow, then.'

Alix was left alone at last. She watched him thread his way through the tables and disappear. And then she turned and gazed once more across the harbour at the rocking boats, the glittering water and the great fort that guarded the seaward entrance to the city of Dubrovnik.

However long she lived, she would never forget this, she thought, totally divorced from the hubbub around her, the babel of languages, the chatter and laughter of a hundred tourists. For in spite of all that had happened here, Dubrovnik had won her heart. It had opened its bastions to her and taken her in; and she would never be quite the same again.

CHAPTER EIGHT

WHEN Alix woke next morning the sky was still the pearly grey of the last hour before dawn. A heavy dusk lay over the smooth pewter sea, and as she watched from her window she could see the faint lightening and the slow colouring of the sky to the east, beyond the old city.

She had had another largely sleepless night. Until now her dreams had been disturbed by the knowledge that Kinnan was close, with only a flimsy partition between them. Tonight had been different. A strange loneliness had invaded her rest. He was not there, and she felt unaccountably bereft.

Restlessly she slipped out of bed and went to look in the mirror. Well, if he'd called her an urchin before there was no knowing what he'd call her now! Huge topaz eyes peered from dark hollows of fatigue. Long brown hair, its golden lights dulled, hung lank around her shoulders. Her body was thin rather than slender, and her slim shoulders drooped.

You'd have more sense if you cut and run now, she told herself severely, instead of hanging about here. Just because you've promised to meet Jon tonight. . . . He'd understand, for goodness' sake. You could send him a note. Why not go, now, while the going's good? There's only pain for you here.

But she was too emotionally and physically exhausted to contemplate packing her clothes yet again, lifting that rucksack on to her back and setting off into the unknown. Too weary to study bus timetables, work out a route, too tired even to make a decision about where to go next. Mostar, Orebic, Korcula, Split . . . the names paraded through her mind like a trail of colourless railway platforms, flat and straight and uninteresting.

As the sun began to colour the landscape she went quietly downstairs to the kitchen. Jon had told her yesterday that breakfast wasn't included in the room price, but that she was welcome to prepare her own food. She had bought a few provisions on the way back yesterday evening and now she made herself a cup of coffee and buttered a roll. Without any real idea of where she was going, she put some lunch and her swimming things into her bag and slipped out of the house before anyone else had appeared.

It was almost inevitable that her footsteps should take her in the direction of the old city. It was almost as if it were a magnet, drawing her into its centre, taking her to its heart for the comfort she so badly needed. She felt now that she knew every yard of it, every narrow alleyway, every terrace and square, every fountain and every flight of steps.

But she was surprised to find the city full of traffic—or at least, comparatively so. Having never seen so much as a moped in the streets, she found it strange to see lorries delivering goods and taking away rubbish. Such things had to be done some time, she realised, and obviously early morning was the best. But the broad Placa seemed a different place when one had to weave between lorries and vans. Instead, she slipped down one of the side streets and made her way along under the wall on the seaward side.

Only yesterday she had been up on the top, she thought, gazing up at the shadowy face of the long wall. Yesterday she had been looking down at the sea far below, frothed with cream as it swirled on the rocks that clutched at the foot of the walls like great stone fists. And even there she had seen people, bathing and lying in the sun. Presumably they had picked their way round from the mole, passing the pool where she had shared lunch with Jon a few days earlier. She could go there today; it would be peaceful, away from the bustle and chatter of the city, and surely no one would find her there.

But when she arrived at the harbour she changed her mind. The boat was already taking on passengers for the island of Lokrum. On a sudden impulse, Alix joined them and squeezed herself on to one of the narrow seats between a group of laughing Yugoslavs. Lokrum was clearly a holiday destination for the locals as well as the tourists—a recommendation in itself.

Alix watched as the boat left the harbour and headed out to the island. The city seemed to withdraw itself, indifferent to the fact that a boatload of people were abandoning it for the day. Closed within its walls, it was completely self-sufficient, and she understood the reassurance this must have given to those who had lived there in medieval times, the security that they must have felt in times that were rocked with uncertainty and danger.

Now they were passing the coastline east of the city, with the hotels that were built into the sloping cliffs; the Argentina and the Excelsior with their broad beaches. Farther along the cliffs rose magnificently and she could see, like a tiny winding ribbon, the road she had travelled with Kinnan on their way from Herceg-Novi. . . .

No! She *must* stop thinking of Kinnan. Stop seeing those grey eyes, the chestnut hair that flowed back from his high forehead, the athletic body; stop hearing the voice that could be tender or harsh; stop feeling the warmth of his kisses, the strength of his arms. . . . Abruptly, she turned to look out on the other side of the boat.

They were running along the northern banks of the island now. Pines and cedars swept almost down to the sea, separated from the water only by a shelf of white and grey rock. As they drew nearer Alix saw people already on the rocks, swimming and fishing. And then the boat turned and made for a small harbour, mooring at the single stone jetty.

Alix joined the queue to disembark and went ashore, looking about her with interest. There was a large board at the top of the jetty, with a map of the island drawn on it. She paused and studied it.

Well, the nudist beach at the end of the island was out for a start! She remembered Kinnan's remarks about this and noticed that a good many people seemed to be taking that particular path; she was quite sure that she could never do such a thing. But there were other beaches on the far side of the island, and a museum and a botanical garden. There seemed to be plenty to see, and after a few moments' further study to impress the map's features on her mind, Alix set off towards the botanical gardens.

But she saw little of the plants, collected from all over the world; the eucalyptus, the flame trees, the giant yuccas all passed before her eyes as if they were dandelions. And although she stopped and studied them all, whatever impressions they made were gone instantly.

Her thoughts were, in spite of all her vows to forget him, almost entirely taken up with the man who had rescued her from her misadventure a few days ago, only to plunge her into even worse disaster; the man who had stolen her lips, her love and her heart. Kinnan Macrae; the man who refused to be forgotten.

The sun rose high and grew hotter. Alix wandered the paths of Lokrum, shielded from its ferocity by the tall scented pines and the spreading cedars. It was quiet and peaceful; now and then she would meet other people, usually in twos or threes, who smiled and nodded, not knowing in which language to greet each other. Occasionally she would come to a gap in the trees and look out over the sea; she saw other islands like a chain disappearing into the distance, and once the ferry-boat making its regular trip to and from Dubrovnik. A yacht under full sail went by like a bird with billowing white wings, and she gazed after it yearningly, thinking sadly that she had never even seen *Manta* under sail, let alone known the motion of the ketch, speeding like an albatross over the waves.

At about one o'clock she became conscious that she was hungry and made her way down to the rocky shore on the southern edge of the island. There were few people here; the better beaches were farther along, but the peace suited Alix's mood and she found a spot where she could sunbathe and eat her lunch, slipping out of her flowered skirt and blouse to stretch out in her bikini, revelling in the warmth of the sun on her skin.

She took very little notice of the motor launch that drifted by, almost silently, half an hour later. And although it was still there when she decided that it would be safe to swim now, she barely gave it a thought as she made her way down to the water's edge, glanced appreciatively into the clear green depths, and slid into the silky coolness. So it came as a complete shock to her, as she swam lazily away from the beach, when she found herself face to face with the man who had haunted her thoughts both awake and asleep, and looked unbelievingly into those cool grey eyes that seemed to know her so uncomfortably well.

'Kinnan!' Her body seemed to freeze, her heart became a hammer pounding in her breast.

'Alix.' His greeting was as composed as hers was agitated, a mere articulation of her name. His tone was indifferent, his eyes cold. He watched her, treading water so that he stayed directly in front of her.

Alix glanced wildly around. Where had he come from? How *could* he have appeared like this, just when

she thought she was safe? She saw the motor launch
and realised that it was the one belonging to *Manta*, the
one she herself had shared with Kinnan when they had
visited the smaller island. She looked back at him, saw
the dangerous glint in his eye, and panicked. With a
twist of her body and a thrust of both feet she was
away, swimming back to the shore with all the speed
she could muster.

Of course, she should have known it was useless.
Almost before she had completed three strokes he was
on her, his hands cruel on her shoulders as he dragged
her round to face him again. Water slapped over her
face as she threshed wildly in an attempt to escape; she
came to the surface fighting and kicking, heard him
swear as one of her feet connected with his shin, then
felt his legs grip hers like rods of iron, preventing any
further movement as he pulled her close into his arms.
Their faces were only inches apart; Kinnan let his body
float to the surface, taking hers with it, and she forced
herself to relax, knowing that they would go under if
she didn't. They lay together on the surface of the water
like lovers.

'Please,' she whispered, her skin tingling with the
contact of his flesh. 'Please, Kinnan, let me go. Why do
you keep haunting me like this? What do you want of
me—why can't you forget me, and let me forget
you?'

'I can't forget you, Alix,' he muttered against her hair
that streamed around him. 'I've tried. . . . You must be
some kind of sea-witch, a Lorelei . . . you've put a spell
on me, and there's only one way I know to break it. . . .'

'No!' But her struggles grew feebler even as his hand
roved over her body, reaching down into the water to
find the softness of her, bringing a whimpering cry to
her lips. She must resist . . . she must . . . but the reason
why faded as she became aware only of his hands,
urgent on her breasts, holding her close to him. She

turned her face and felt his lips on hers, parting hers
before their onslaught; trailing fire down her throat to
the nipple that somehow seemed free of any covering.
At the discovery Alix felt a surge of desire and she
pressed herself against him, twining her body about his,
using all her skill to keep herself afloat with him. She
heard him give a grunt of satisfaction and felt his hands
easing the lower part of her bikini. An exquisite agony
flooded through her; she moaned faintly and clung to
him, unable to make any move, aware that she was now
a dragging weight on him but quite incapable of giving
any help in staying above the surface; wanting to
drown, if only in his love.

'My God!' she heard him mutter thickly. 'Alix, we've
got to get aboard the launch.' She felt him turn on his
back, cradling her in his arms, his hands firm on her
breasts, driving with powerful strokes of his legs
through the softly lapping water. The movement of his
body against hers drove her to a fresh frenzy; she
reached her arms above her head, stroking his face with
her palms, felt him turn his lips to kiss her fingers. And
then they were beside the launch and he was helping her
into it, and now the fact that they were both naked
didn't seem to matter any more, and she revelled in the
sensation of the warm sun on her wet, bare skin.

Kinnan scrambled aboard after her and with
trembling fingers he spread a rug on the floor of the
cockpit. He pulled some cushions from a locker and
scattered them on the rug, then he laid Alix very gently
on them and leaned over her. His eyes were dark, the
same smoky grey that had twisted her heart in so many
of her dreams, and his lips were grave and unsmiling.

'This is the point of no return,' he said. 'You know
that, don't you?'

Alix nodded. She still felt faint with desire. She
reached up, linked her hands behind his neck, wanting
to draw him down, wanting him to love her. But he

resisted her and stayed above her, watching her face, searching her eyes.

'You are sure, Alix?' he asked, his voice rough. 'Because I can't stand much more of this. It's now or never—but if you'd rather it was never, you've got to say and say quickly. I'll respect that . . . but oh, God, it's going to be hell—for both of us.' He searched her face and then traced a line from brow to chin. 'You want me as much as I want you, don't you, Alix?'

Alix nodded dumbly. Whatever happened afterwards, this was something that was as inevitable as sunset. Perhaps it had always been inevitable, right from the start; perhaps that was why they'd been unable to part, why each attempt of hers to leave had been foiled, why even now he had found her. She didn't know, was past caring about whether they were right to let their desire have its way; all she knew was that having fought so long, she could fight no longer. Afterwards would have to take care of itself.

'Love me, Kinnan,' she whispered, her voice a tiny thread of sound. 'Please—please love me. . . .'

She saw the stern face above her relax and soften, first with relief and then a strange tenderness. And then it grew taut again, taut with a desire more powerful than any she had seen before. Her own longing rose to match it and she dragged his head down to hers, found his lips and lifted her body to meet his. She never knew who it was that groaned then; the sound seemed to be forced out of them both, and then their bodies took over, making love with a desperate urgency born of the frustration that had been between them ever since their first kiss—a few days, a lifetime or a century ago? Inexperience, Alix found, was no handicap; it was as if her limbs had always known how to twine around his, her lips had always known how to return his kisses, and, as he gave her one final burning glance before his body covered hers and they came together in a starburst of passion, it was as if her body were welcoming a lover it had known long, long before; the crescendo of her love was a revelation of delight, yet somehow as familiar as if she had been waiting for it all her life.

At last they lay softly entwined, their breathing slowly steadying, their heartbeats returning to normal. And Alix, wrapped close in his arms, looked up at the blazing sky and wondered why they had fought each other for so long; how they could have done so when there was all this happiness waiting. She turned in his arms, kissed him softly and ran her hand down the length of his body.

'No regrets?' he murmured into her hair.

'No regrets,' she returned, and nestled closer against him, marvelling at the apparent bonelessness of his body. Before, he had seemed all hardness and strength; now, relaxed, his body was as soft and supple as her own and their contours merged as if they flowed into each other. She sighed as he kissed her with a gentleness that was a sharp contrast to the passion that had whirled them to a pinnacle of bliss such a short time before.

At last Kinnan stirred. He had drawn a large towel over them to protect them from the sun; now he sat up and the towel fell away, revealing his broad, tanned chest. Alix opened her eyes sleepily, reached up and touched it with her fingers.

'You know what you've done to me, Alix?' he murmured, his eyes watching her gravely. 'You've done what I swore no woman would ever do . . . you've made me fall in love with you.'

Alix smiled. A new confidence seemed to flow through her body. 'You're not complaining, are you?'

'No, I'm not complaining,' he said softly. 'I just have to rearrange my entire life, that's all. I told you there was no room in it for you . . . and now I find that without you it's all pointless anyway.' He lay down

again, pressing himself close to her. 'I should have
known from the start—or at least from the day we went
diving. They warn you about this at diving school, you
know. Rapture of the Deep, it's called. Only *they* told
me it was something that happened if you went deeper
than a hundred feet and still used air to breathe—it's
the nitrogen in the air that does it. Its proper name is
nitrogen narcosis. What they didn't tell me——' he
kissed her, a long deep kiss that left her gasping '—was
that it can happen even on the surface. In certain
conditions——' he kissed her again '—and in the right
company. . . .'

They lay silent, their hearts pulsing strongly together.
The same half-familiar weakness was invading Alix's
body and she moved languorously against him. But
Kinnan smiled against her cheek and moved away. He
sat up again, his hand cupping her breast.

'So what are we going to do?' he asked. 'How do I
rearrange my life, Alix, to include you—and marriage?'

'Marriage?' she repeated. 'You—you want to marry
me, Kinnan?' and was surprised by the look almost of
anger that crossed his face, creasing his fine brows and
making a hard line of his mouth.

'Well, what did you *think* I wanted?' he demanded. 'I
told you the other day, I don't go in for seducing
innocent young virgins. What we did just now
committed us, you understand? Or maybe you didn't
realise that?'

'I didn't realise anything,' she confessed. 'Only——'
She stopped and felt herself blush as he smiled.

'Well, I did,' he told her. 'Alix, just what kind of a
louse did you think I was? Did you think I'd just shrug
my shoulders when I found you'd gone? Did you think
I'd just say to hell with it, the one that got away—and
go back to playing the field? Not that I ever did much
of that—a lot of what I said to you was just talk. But I
won't pretend there haven't been one or two. Not any

more, though, you can take my word for that. From this moment on, I'm a one-woman man.' He lifted her against him. 'So when do we get married, Alix my love? Because I won't rest easy until I've got that golden band safely on your finger!'

'I—I don't know!' She stared at him, confused. 'We—we'll have to go back to England, won't we? *Can* we get married here? And there's my parents—and your family too. I don't even know if you have one! Kinnan——'

'All right,' he said. 'I can see we need to sort out a few things first. And I'm not sure what the position is about getting married here. I've never really had to wonder about it before!' He pulled on his shorts and smiled at her. 'Delectable though you look, my sweet, I really think I'd better go and rescue your clothes—can't take you back to *Manta* like that!' He put his finger to her lips. 'Don't go away, will you!'

Alix watched as he swam with steady strokes to the shore and collected her clothes. He slipped them into a waterproof bag he had taken with him and then swam back.

She leaned her chin on her palm, thinking contentedly how things had changed, and how swiftly. Somehow everything seemed different now—as if the world had shifted slightly so that she saw everything from a different angle. As if a distorting mirror had been replaced by a perfect one, so that reflections that had seemed twisted and ugly now appeared pure and true. With Kinnan's love still glowing inside her, she knew that all her doubts had been swept away, her scruples forgotten. And although there might still be some things that should be explained, there would be no more difficulty over them.

'Kinnan,' she said when she was dressed again and they were sitting close in the stern of the boat as he steered it slowly round the island, 'I'm sorry I was so prickly before. I was wrong, I know that now. But I've always had this distrust of money—and when I realised you were so rich it turned me against you. I couldn't help it—but I realise now that it isn't your fault you were born to rich parents. It doesn't really make any difference to *you*.'

Kinnan was silent for a few moments. His arm round her was warm and strong. Then he looked down at her and his eyes glinted with laughter as he said: 'You never cease to surprise me, Alix. Why are you so against money? I can think of a lot of girls who would find it no deterrent at all!'

'Yes, I know,' she answered soberly. 'But you see, I have a reason. . . .' She hesitated, choosing her words. 'I had a brother once—Stephen. He was quite a few years older than I was and I suppose Mum and Dad had spoilt him a bit, thinking he was going to be the only one. He was good-looking and clever and charming. Everyone liked him, he made friends easily—too easily. And when he won a lot of money on a lottery ticket that he'd only bought for a joke—well, he made the wrong kind of friends, I suppose. He was at university then, but from that moment he seemed to go haywire. He stopped working, lived for the moment; spent his money like water.'

She stopped, her hazel eyes brimming with tears. Kinnan waited for a moment and then said gently: 'And then?'

She shrugged. 'It all ended quite suddenly. He'd got this new car—a sports model, very fast. He—he hit a tree one night . . . they said he couldn't have known a thing about it. . . .' Her voice broke, and Kinnan tightened his arm.

'Yes, that's tough. And how old were you at the time?'

'Thirteen.'

'So it made quite an impression on you, didn't it?

You'd have been at the age to hero-worship this clever, good-looking brother of yours. It must have come as quite a shock to find he had feet of clay after all—especially on top of losing him that way.'

'Feet of clay?' Alix repeated doubtfully.

Kinnan looked at her. He seemed to be assessing her; considering whether or not to say what was in his mind. But he clearly decided that this was not the time. Instead, he bent and kissed her lightly.

'We'll talk about it again some time. Just now I'm more interested in our future than our pasts. I'm going to take you into Dubrovnik as soon as we get back and buy you that engagement ring. That'll be a start. And then we'll make enquiries about getting married. You may be right—we may have to go back to England. Or would you want to anyway?'

'I think my parents would like it,' Alix began, then looked at him and smiled. 'But if it means waiting while you go to the Great Barrier Reef and the Caribbean and all those other exotic places you want to film, well. . . .'

Kinnan laughed. 'It won't mean that,' he assured her. 'I don't intend waiting a moment longer than necessary! No, if we have to go back we'll make a flying visit and get a special licence. You can share your day with your family then, if that's what you want.'

'And yours?' she asked timidly. 'Your family, I mean.'

'No problem there,' he answered briefly. 'I don't have any.' Then he turned away from her and began to point out features of interest on the Lapad peninsula, and Alix realised that she still had a lot to learn about the man she loved . . . that was, if he intended teaching her. . . .

The rest of the day passed in a haze of happiness. Neither Jon nor Vita were aboard *Manta* when they arrived, and for the first time since the day Vita had

arrived, they had the ketch to themselves. Alix
wandered around it, feeling almost as if she had come
home, delighting in the familiarity of the saloon, the
luxurious fittings that in no way detracted from the
practical seaworthiness of the vessel. Kinnan clearly
liked his comfort, but not at the expense of his sailing,
and she realised that this preference chimed in with his
whole attitude to life, a kind of ruggedness that gave
new quality to the surface urbanity, like the muscles
that rippled under the silk shirt he wore in the evenings.

Once or twice she wondered what would happen
when Vita discovered that they had come together
again. The beautiful journalist's threats nagged at her
mind and she almost mentioned her worries to Kinnan.
But she could not find it in her heart to bring an
unsavoury note into their magic day. Let us have this,
she thought, before the trouble starts. Because trouble
there would be, she was sure. And she was equally sure
that Kinnan would be able to deal with it.

'Do you mind if I do some work for an hour or two?'
Kinnan asked, half apologetically. 'I want to write up
some notes on what we did yesterday, and there's Jon's
work with the aquarium curator to be assessed too. It
won't take me long, but I'd like to get it out of the way.
You can sunbathe on deck and turn all the other
yachtsmen green with envy. And I'll send someone to
the house where you were staying to settle up and
collect your clothes.'

'Of course I don't mind,' said Alix, and she lay on the
roof of the deckhouse, roasting gently, while Kinnan
worked just below her. It was a warm, companionable
feeling, she thought, peering down at his bent head and
loving the wave of his russet hair, the smooth tan of his
naked back. It must be like this being married. And for
the rest of the afternoon she gave herself up to a rosy
daydream of just what married life was going to be like,
with Kinnan.

As the sun went down, casting its coppery glow over the placid water, he rose, flexed his muscles and announced that he'd finished. 'And now we're going to dress up and go and buy your ring and celebrate our engagement,' he declared. 'Put on that Yugoslavian thing you wore the other night—I liked that.'

'Well, you could have said so!' she protested, laughing. 'I felt a real country bumpkin beside Vita, and I thought that was what you thought too.'

'Nonsense! You looked fresh and lovely. Vita was ludicrously overdressed as usual.' He caught her to him and looked into her eyes. 'You're to stop thinking of yourself as a nobody, Alix, do you understand? You're a wonderful, lovely girl and I'm lucky to have found you. Just remember that.'

'I can't forget it,' she said softly. 'Even though I can't really believe it either. I love you, Kinnan.'

'And I love you.' His arms tightened and for a moment Alix wondered if they were ever going to get to the old city that night. Then he let go, smiling a little shakily. 'I'm not going to kiss you now, Alix, so it's no use looking at me with those huge green eyes of yours. If I touch you again I'll never let you go—and I do want to buy you that ring!'

Laughing, they went below to change. Alix washed her long hair again to get the salt out, brushing it out to lie on her shoulders, and slipped into the Yugoslavian outfit. It did suit her; the other night she had felt ill at ease under Vita's amused and patronising stare, but now she looked into her mirror and saw a slender girl who glowed with happiness, radiating a new confidence that seemed to give her added inches, her figure an added richness, her hair an added shine. For the first time she felt a complete person. It was as if for her whole life she had been only half there, searching for the partner that would make her whole. And now she had found him.

And Dubrovnik seemed a different city tonight; light and bright, the dark canopy of the sky making a velvet awning over the gaiety of the ancient streets. As they passed through Pile they found a group of middle-aged Slovenians, here to celebrate some war-time anniversary, holding an impromptu concert under a tree, their voices blending in a harmony that, even though she could not understand the words, brought a lump to Alix's throat. Inside the city there was more music; this time from two young buskers seated on the steps of Onofrio's fountain. The star of the two was clearly the violinist, a thin youth with dark hair and liquid eyes whose instrument seemed to be a part of him. His friend, a guitarist, was simply backing him as they played a selection of Yugoslav dance tunes, moved on into pop that they gave a flavour entirely their own and then progressed to classical music. With delight, Alix recognised Tchaikovsky's violin concerto and she stood rapt by Kinnan's side, warmly encircled by his arm, as the young violinist took them through the slow movement while the guitarist sat back on his stone seat, content to let his friend take the acclaim. It seemed only moments before it was all over, yet when Alix moved she found her limbs stiff from having stood so still.

'Wasn't it wonderful!' She looked up at Kinnan with shining eyes. 'We must give him something.' But Kinnan was already taking out some notes, and she warmed to his generosity.

'A boy who can play like that deserves encouragement,' he said as they walked away, listening this time to the fading strains of a guitar solo. 'I didn't realise you liked music, Alix.'

'Oh yes, it means a lot to me. I can't do much myself, though I learned to play the piano—just enough for school things and to amuse myself. But I love listening to it.'

'I'll take you to one of the concerts in the Rector's Palace,' he offered. 'Pity there isn't one on tonight.'

'Oh no—we've had our music tonight. It was magic. And ... there's everything else as well.' Her smile was shy, but he caught her meaning and sent her a look of tenderness, before turning aside to look into a jeweller's shop that was still open.

The choice of a ring took a long time. Alix was relieved to find that Kinnan, although apparently prepared to spend what seemed to her to be an exorbitant sum, was not insistent that she have anything elaborate or showy. That wouldn't suit her, he agreed. But it had to be good. And she ended up with an exquisitely-wrought ring of modern design, the gold fashioned in its own intricate pattern around the single diamond. It suited Alix's slender hand to perfection, and as she gazed at it her eyes misted over with tears. It seemed to be a symbol of so much; of the love that had grown between her and Kinnan and refused to be denied; of the tenderness and cherishing that wove itself like a bright thread of gold through his passionate loving; and of the integrity that shone like the diamond in the centre of his heart.

There was nothing that words could say. Only her eyes could express what this moment meant to her, and their message seemed to satisfy Kinnan, for his own were as eloquent. And they left the shop and walked along the Placa hand in hand, silent, in a tiny world of their own among the throng of people; in a magic world where words were not needed and the slightest touch could say it all.

Kinnan took her to a small restaurant for dinner. They went up stone steps and sat on a terrace above the street, looking down through plants and vines to the people who passed below. The tables were lit by fat candles and soft music played in the background. Alix ate dreamily, hardly aware of anything but that it was all delicious; she drank the wine Kinnan offered her and they talked in low voices, making crazy plans for the future. They would sail the world in *Manta*, he said, visiting all the places he needed for his film, as well as others he had seen for himself and wanted to show her. He would teach her to dive and take her down with him so that they could share the beauty—as well as the rapture, he added with a grin—of the deep. And one day they would return to England and live somewhere in the country, making nature films and bringing up their own family to love and enjoy the beauty that was everywhere around them.

A tiny needle of doubt pricked at Alix when he said that. What was going to happen about Vita? she wondered. And Vita's father—Max Purvis, the man who owned the TV company in which Kinnan had hoped to become a partner. What would be his reaction when he discovered that Kinnan was not after all to be his son-in-law? Would it wreck their plans? Would it spell the end of Kinnan's hopes and ambitions?

As they walked back to *Manta* at last, slowly as if each was reluctant to bring their magic evening to an end, Alix was coldly aware that she might very soon find out. For presumably Vita too would be returning to *Manta*. And she shivered to think of the other girl's reaction to their news. It could, she thought, be very unpleasant indeed.

To Alix's relief, however, the ketch was still deserted when she and Kinnan returned through the soft darkness, their arms still wound round each other. They climbed aboard and stood in the shadow of the deckhouse, close together, rocking gently with the movement of the boat.

'I don't want tonight to end,' she murmured at last against Kinnan's lips.

'Neither do I, my sweet. But I think we must say goodnight now. You're dropping on your feet. And I'd quite like to be out of the way before the others come back.'

She looked up at him, her eyes wide and questioning, and he added: 'In our own cabins, I think, don't you? We don't want to risk the magic spell being spoilt.'

Clearly he too expected trouble from Vita, and Alix nodded. She longed to spend the night held close in Kinnan's arms; but the sharing of their love that afternoon had shown her that passion, once aroused, took no heed of discretion. And to make love with Kinnan while Vita was on board would be totally impossible.

She let him guide her gently into her own cabin and kiss her goodnight before closing the door. Still bemused, still enchanted, she undressed and slipped into bed. And although she felt no desire for sleep, wanting only to lie awake and relive the events of the day, almost as soon as she lay down her eyes closed. She heard no more; neither Jon's return, nor Vita's; nor the sounds of early morning that had previously woken her so effectively.

CHAPTER NINE

'So you're back!'

The words cut like ice through the shimmering air of early morning. Still dazed with sleep, Alix raised her head from her pillow and stared at the girl who stood in the doorway. Her heart sank. Vita was looking her most aggressive in a scarlet shirt and jeans, her figure like a flame and her eyes flashing fire.

'I thought we'd seen the back of you,' Vita went on, advancing into the cabin. 'Oh, I knew Kinnan was pretty wild when he discovered you'd gone—but as I told you before, I thought it was just a passing thing and he'd get over it. After all, I was here to help him. But it seems I was wrong.' She stood over the bed, towering over Alix as she lay there. 'You think you've done very well, don't you? Playing hard to get, till you had him almost out of his mind—and then snap! Your little trap closed and you'd caught him. Or so you thought!' The sneer was unmistakable, and Alix felt a flash of anger.

'It wasn't like that!' she retorted. 'But even if it had been, is it any of your business? Kinnan's a grown man, an adult, and he doesn't belong to you. He makes his own decisions, or hadn't you realised that? And since he's asked me to marry him I don't see that what he does has any more to do with you!'

'Asked you to marry him!' Vita's lip curled. 'That's a laugh! And did he bare his soul to you—tell you all? Or is he still a mystery man, taking you for the same ride he took all the others? I tell you, little schoolmarm, that man's a tangle of secrets—and only I know the truth about him. The truth I'm willing to stake my job he still hasn't told you!'

'Told me—what?' A cold finger touched Alix's heart.

Vita's dark eyes glinted with triumph and Alix realised that whatever it was the older girl was about to tell her was going to change everything. Desperately, she wished that she need not hear it; that she could cover her ears and refuse to listen. But that would, she knew, be no use. If there were to be any love between Kinnan and herself, any hope of a lifelong relationship, she had to know.

Vita laughed, a low, unpleasant laugh that sent shivers down Alix's spine. 'He hasn't told you, has he! Somehow I didn't think he would. . . . But I really think you ought to know, little innocent. So that you realise just what you're letting yourself in for . . . just what risks you're taking . . . just what kind of a man Kinnan Macrae is. . . .'

'All right!' Alix shouted at her. 'Tell me! Tell me whatever it is—tell me everything you know—and then get out! It won't make any difference.'

'Won't it? I wonder.' The journalist closed the door. 'I doubt if we'll be overheard—Kinnan's gone over to the harbourmaster's office and Jon's gone in to Dubrovnik. You want to know all about Kinnan, then, do you? Well, little one, here it is—but don't blame me if it's all too much for you.'

Alix watched as Vita settled herself indolently on the end of the berth. The beautiful face was hard, the lustrous eyes cold as she surveyed her victim. A tiny smile played about her lips. She's actually *enjoying* this, Alix thought suddenly. Like a cat, playing with a mouse.

'Kinnan's never mentioned Alison to you, I suppose?' Vita said suddenly.

'Alison? No.' Bewilderment clouded Alix's mind.

'As I thought. He never mentions her to anyone—and with good reason. Because Alison's story is rather a tragic one, and it was all due to Kinnan.' She got up abruptly. 'He couldn't have been more responsible for her death if he'd held a gun to her head.'

'Her *death*? *Kinnan*—what are you saying?' Alix felt as if all the blood had drained from her body. A shuddering cold enveloped her and she drew the bedclothes round her, staring with wide horrified eyes at Vita.

'Oh, he didn't actually *kill* her—not directly.' The girl's laugh was short and unmusical. 'But he drove her to it.' She turned and looked directly into Alix's face, and Alix stared back, mesmerised. 'He and Alison were having an affair, you see. Had been for years, on and off. She was older than him—old enough to be his mother, just about. A rich widow—yes, sordid, isn't it? She'd known him since he was a kid, always been good to him. I suppose he thought he'd make sure of a good thing. He had to have money to do what he wanted, and she had it.'

'But so did he, surely,' Alix said faintly.

'What gave you that idea? Kinnan's family were as poor as church mice. He never had a couple of pennies to rub together. But he had ambition and he had talent, and it was well known that Alison helped him, gave him a start. He just wasn't satisfied, that was all—so he gave her ideas.'

'I don't believe it,' Alix whispered, and Vita laughed that unpleasant, jeering laugh again.

'Yes, you do. It all fits in, doesn't it? Poor artist, rich patron—it's happened time and time again. Well, it got to the point where he was living with her. I suppose she thought he was going to marry her, poor cow. She even made a will leaving everything to him. And then, one fine afternoon when Kinnan was off on one of his trips, making a film—some tinpot schools thing—she must have come to terms with the fact that he was never going to marry her, that she was about to lose him. He was going around with someone else by then and I guess she heard about it.' Vita paused, watching Alix almost greedily. 'She took an overdose and went to bed. By the time she was found, it was too late.'

'Too late!' Alix breathed. She gazed out of the porthole, seeing instead of the shining sea a luxurious bedroom somewhere; a bed where a woman slept, her face marked with tears, her arms flung wide to welcome the lover she would never see again. . . . And all for money. All for ambition; greed. Another life wasted, and all because of money. Alison . . . Stephen . . . there seemed to be little difference between them.

Why hadn't Kinnan told her he'd been poor, she wondered, why had he let her think he'd always been rich? And she knew the answer at once. Because he would have had to explain how he became the owner of a luxury yacht, the partner in a TV company, able to travel the world with the finest equipment. And he had known her well enough to realise what her reaction would have been.

I could have forgiven him almost anything, she thought sadly. Anything but that.

She became aware that Vita was watching her, narrow-eyed. Waiting for a reaction, no doubt. Well, she would spare her the satisfaction of a scene. This was a matter between Kinnan and herself.

'Thank you for telling me,' she said, her voice small but steady. 'I think I'll get up now. Kinnan's gone to the harbourmaster's office, you say? I'll walk along and meet him.'

'Is that all you're going to say?' Vita's tone was vicious. 'You mean you actually condone Kinnan's behaviour? Or maybe you don't care how he came by his money! Maybe you're as unscrupulous as he is!'

'I didn't say that,' Alix replied quietly. 'But I have to see Kinnan—I have to speak to him. It wouldn't be fair to—to run away again, without hearing his point of view.'

'In other words, you don't believe me—or maybe you do, but you want to hear his lies, you want to have something else to believe, so that you can pretend. Oh, you're all the same, you so-called innocents—you can't bear life as it is, so you build up a framework of lies and pretence to help you get through—so that you can justify your own feelings, so that you can love someone like Kinnan and pretend his faults just don't exist.'

'That's not true! And if Kinnan is so bad, why are you worrying anyway? Why do *you* want him so badly?'

Vita smiled, a glittering catlike smile. 'Because I'm different from you, little Miss Prim. I can see Kinnan for what he is and accept him. I don't love him, you see—not the way you think you do. But I know that he and I could have a good life together—in bed and out of it. Kinnan Macrae's got a lot of things I want. And I mean to have them—and him.'

'Isn't that for him to decide?' Alix asked coolly, though inside she was shaking with distress. 'At the moment he seems to prefer me.'

Vita snapped her fingers dismissively. 'A passing madness, that's all. It wouldn't last.' She came closer, laid a long hand on Alix's arm. 'I tell you, I'm doing you a favour. Kinnan could only make you unhappy. You just aren't his weight. Remember what happened to Alison.'

Alix controlled her distaste at the feeling of the long red fingernails on her skin and moved away. Her heart was thundering, but she was determined not to let the other girl see how upset she was. Her thoughts chased themselves round her mind. Was it true? It was something that could be checked—would Vita have risked telling her a completely fabricated story? Surely Kinnan would be able to tell her the truth, set her mind at rest.

But what could the truth be? Vita had told her he had lived with Alison; she'd gone so far as to make her will in his favour. And then, afraid that he was about to abandon her, she'd killed herself. What other explanation could there be?

Vita was watching her. Somehow, Alix had to get rid of the other girl. She wouldn't be able to control herself much longer, she knew. And she could not bear to let Vita see how badly hurt she was.

'All right,' she said in a low voice. 'You've told me enough. I'm getting up now. And then——'

'And then?'

'I shall see Kinnan and tell him what you've told me.' Alix's voice was firm. 'I have to. I have to give him a chance at least.'

Vita's face changed. The gloating triumph left her eyes and was replaced by a malevolence so spiteful that Alix shrank away. Her beautiful lips drew back to bare sharp white teeth. Her skin seemed to tighten so that the bone structure of her cheeks and forehead stood out like a skull.

'You will *not* see Kinnan!' she rasped. 'I'm having no more of this—you've spoilt everything since you came here, you interfering little prig. Have to give him a chance indeed! What chances do *I* get? I've been planning things for Kinnan Macrae for years, and I'm not having you wreck everything just at the last moment!' She stood up and to Alix's horrified eyes she looked like some kind of demon, in her brilliant red outfit and with her eyes flashing with rage. 'No, little schoolmistress, you will *not* see Kinnan—and I'll tell you why.' Bending down, she brought her face close to Alix, who pressed herself back against the pillows, cringing from the other girl's nearness. 'Because I was on Lokrum yesterday—and I had my camera with me!'

For a moment the full meaning of this failed to get through to Alix. On Lokrum—with her camera? And then she realised, and closed her eyes as a sudden nausea swept over her.

'I never thought you'd really gone, you see, in spite of what Jon said,' Vita went on gloatingly. 'So I asked a few questions—oh, so cleverly, he never knew what he was telling me—and I found out enough to have a good idea of where you might be. And knowing your habit of getting up early, I was around in time to see you leave. It was easy then to follow you—and very, very worthwhile. Did you enjoy your spot of nude bathing? I was quite surprised—you're not nearly as prim and proper as you led us to believe, are you?'

'No!' Alix breathed. 'No—you didn't! Oh, you couldn't——'

'But I did. And I very easily could.' Vita was triumphant again. 'I saw you gambolling there in the water like dolphins—such a pretty, romantic sight. It will make some very good photographs.' She paused, and her eyes flicked over Alix's white face.

'You—you wouldn't. . . .' Alix whispered at last.

'Wouldn't I? Do you really want to take that chance? Remember, I have contacts. I even have my own gossip column.' Another pause. 'It could just about finish Kinnan. And as for you—well, the governors of your school might think again about just who they want on their staff. . . .'

Alix covered her face with her hands. Everything Vita said was true. For Kinnan's sake—for her own, for her parents'—she couldn't let those photos appear. Whatever the price.

'What do you want me to do?' she asked at last, her voice flat.

Vita shrugged. 'Simple. Just be on your way—without seeing Kinnan. You've just got time to pack. I'll get you a taxi. And this time, don't come back.'

'Why do you hate me so much?' Alix breathed, and Vita laughed.

'My dear child, I don't hate you! No more than I'd hate a spider or a wasp—you're just an irritant. Rather a persistent one, though—so naturally I have to take steps to remove you. Just as I'd squash a spider or a wasp.'

'You have no real feelings, do you?'

'I try not to, if by real feelings you mean the kind of sloppy sentimentality most people seem to go in for. So far as I can see, all that leads to is trouble. It's much better to keep a clear head. Don't forget what I said about those arranged marriages. They work!'

Alix sighed. She and Vita lived in different worlds, worlds that would never meet. But she could not think about that now. All she could think was that she must leave *Manta*—and Kinnan—and leave quickly, before the numbness faded and the pain began.

'I'll leave you to pack,' said Vita, moving over to the door. 'Don't be too long, will you—we've spent longer on this than I expected.'

It was like a nightmare, Alix thought as she got into the taxi on the quay. A recurrent nightmare. It had all happened before—her leaving, with Vita's encouragement. The last time hadn't been final after all, though she'd meant it to be. This time was. It had to be—for so many reasons.

'Hey!'

She twisted round in sudden panic as the shout echoed across the quay, rising above all the other sounds. Running footsteps accompanied it and Alix saw Kinnan racing towards her. She leaned forward and tapped the driver urgently on the shoulder, making frantic gestures at him to hurry; but he stared back uncomprehendingly and she knew that her efforts were only holding them up.

'Please—please hurry—*vite—schnell*—oh dear! *Why* didn't I learn any Serbo-Croat?'

But it was no use. The taxi-driver, with one final bewildered look at her, let in the clutch at last—just as Kinnan reached the car and grabbed at the door.

'Alix! What the hell are you doing?' His eyes took in the scarlet rucksack. 'Oh, my God, not again! What's got into you *this* time? Look, we can't talk like this—get out of that damned taxi!'

The driver expostulated and Kinnan dragged some notes from his pocket, thrusting them impatiently through the window with a few curt words of explanation. Alix could almost see the taxi-driver thinking *mad English*—but he shrugged and pocketed the money, leaning back over the seat to pass the rucksack out as Kinnan wrenched Alix's door open and pulled her out.

'Please——' Alix began. 'No—don't go——' But the taxi was already drawing away and she struggled futilely against Kinnan's iron strength.

'And now perhaps we can have an explanation,' Kinnan said grimly. 'Just what are you playing at, Alix? Is this some kind of a joke? Because I don't think it's a very good one.'

'No, Kinnan, it's not a joke.' Alix glanced around, uncomfortably aware of the market close by, the interested stares of passers-by. 'Kinnan, we can't talk here. Anyway, there's nothing to talk about, I——'

'Like hell there's not! All right, we'll go back to *Manta*——'

'*No!*' Panic edged Alix's voice. 'No, please, Kinnan, not to *Manta*. I couldn't——'

'You *what?*' He glanced across with suspicious eyes and Alix followed his glance to see Vita standing on the deck watching them. Oh, dear God, she thought, what now? Would Vita carry out her threat—would she think that Alix had engineered this meeting in defiance of her? There was only one thing to do—she had to convince the watching journalist that she really meant to leave. And she had to make Kinnan angry. Angrier than he was already.

Her heart quailed at the thought, but there was

nothing else for it. She could *not* allow those photographs to appear. She could *not* let Vita wreck Kinnan's career, to say nothing of her parents' happiness. Her own scarcely came into her considerations; that had been wrecked already. All she could do was ensure that the ruin didn't spread to those she loved.

'It's no use, Kinnan,' she panted. 'I can't marry you. It's all over. I should never have stayed here yesterday—I should never have gone to Lokrum. It's been one great, ghastly mistake all the way along the line!'

'Mistake?' he gritted. 'Yesterday was a mistake? That's not what you said last night. I thought I heard you use words like divine—magic—wonderful. I thought I heard you say something about love.'

'I was wrong,' she stammered. 'I didn't know then—I didn't know the truth about you.' She glanced frantically around and saw a bus coming along the quay. For a split second, Kinnan's grip on her eased—and in that second Alix twisted like an eel, wrenched herself free and sprinted for the bus, grabbing at her rucksack as she went.

'*Alix!*' He was close behind her, but she leapt aboard the bus just before his hand could close on her shoulder. 'Alix, what are you babbling about? What truth? Who's been getting at you—you've got to tell me!'

Alix turned on the step and looked at him, then past him to *Manta*, where Vita was still on deck, watching. Well, at least she'd know Alix had really gone this time. And no doubt she would be able to give Kinnan the consolation he needed.

'What truth?' he repeated as the bus drew jerkily away and the doors began to close.

'About Alison!' she screamed at him through the narrowing gap. 'The truth about your money—the truth about *you*!'

Her last glimpse of him was of an expression more furiously angry than she had ever seen before. Shaking, she found a seat and sat down, oblivious of the stares of other passengers. If looks could kill, she thought, and shivered. Maybe Vita had been right. Kinnan *was* the sort of man who could drive a woman to her death. He could give her heaven . . . and hell.

She had had the heaven yesterday; now she braced herself for the hell.

After a while, she began to take note of where she was. She had had no idea where the bus was heading, had just handed the driver a few hundred-dinar notes and taken her change and ticket without bothering much about her destination. But she was heading west, which was fortunate; she had no wish to go back to Herceg-Novi or Kotor, with their memories of the beginning of her adventure. And although she felt that her interest in continuing the tour planned with Bernie wasn't much greater, there didn't seem to be anything else to do. The thought of going straight back to England didn't appeal at all; she needed some respite to lick her wounds.

The bus was following the long inlet into the mountains, the rugged terrain making any journey longer than the average crow would find it. She gazed out of the window, trying to take pleasure in the coastal views, the tiny fishing villages far below, the emerald islands dotted in the sparkling turquoise of the sea. But her former delight had gone; the colours seemed to be dimmed, the sparkle dulled. And her heart, which had seemed light and free yesterday, was now as heavy as a lump of concrete.

There was no doubt of Kinnan's reaction to her final thrust about Alison. She was certain that if she had still been near enough, he would have struck her—or worse. If ever a man looked murderous at that moment, she thought with a shudder, Kinnan had.

And why should he have looked like that if it hadn't been true? If he hadn't wanted it kept a secret from her. If he hadn't known what her reaction would be.

Money, she thought miserably. It all boils down to money. Just like everything else. Oh, why is it so important? Why do people *let* it become important? More important even than love . . . than happiness.

Even here in Yugoslavia, a country where everyone was supposed to be equal, the same thing happened. She looked out at the villages they passed, seeing the poverty of some of the dwellings, the luxury of others. Everyone was entitled to a State home, she'd been told, but those who could afford to build their own were allowed to do so. Everyone was entitled to a minimum standard of living. Yet there were old women trudging back from the fields, their backs bowed under the great sheaves of grasses they were bringing for animal feed; old men leading mules and donkeys; oxen working in the fields. It didn't tie up with the luxury hotels and the expensive goods in Dubrovnik. Or with the expensive yachts that moored along the quay at Gruz.

But who was to say that the old women with their loads or the men with their donkeys weren't happier than those who had to struggle to maintain their higher standard of living? Money hadn't brought happiness to Stephen. Until he had had it, he had been like any other student, hard-working but ready to enjoy himself, looking forward to a useful life. What had gone wrong? Couldn't he have a useful life *with* money, as well as without it?

She knew that the answer must be yes. So was the fault in the money that had come so easily—or had it been in Stephen himself?

Alix had never asked herself this question before, but now she faced it honestly. Stephen hadn't *had* to do the things he did—spend his money so recklessly, forget his work and ambitions, throw himself into a way of life that could only spell disaster. He hadn't had to buy that new car that could go so fast; he hadn't had to drive it recklessly after drinking too much at a party. . . .

Restlessly, she turned to look out of the other window. The bus was almost empty now and she could see across its width to the mountains that lay inland. And she saw that the bus was now crossing a narrow neck of land, so that water lay on both sides. She got out the map she had bought in Dubrovnik and realised that they must be approaching Ston, on the way to Orebic.

Well, Orebic was as good a place to go as any. From there, she could cross the narrow strait to the island of Korcula. She and Bernie had intended going there—and perhaps in a different place she might be able to start pulling her life together again, mending the shreds and tatters it had been left in by Kinnan Macrae.

At Ston, the bus stopped and the driver got down and went into a café. Alix discovered that she was thirsty too—and hungry. She followed, keeping a wary eye on him so that she shouldn't get left behind, and bought a pastry that resembled a sausage roll but turned out to be sweet, and a bottle of lemonade, feeling better when they got back on board the bus.

Ston looked quite an interesting place. She consulted her guide book. A long stone wall encircled the village, reaching high into the hills to include pasture and olive groves, and there were oyster beds in the bay. Perhaps she could stay longer here on her way back, unless she went on to one of the other islands from Korcula. For a moment, she toyed with the idea of staying here now, but dismissed it. It wouldn't be too difficult for Kinnan to find out where the bus had been heading, and he could easily follow her; a lone English girl would be quickly remembered in these quiet places. It would be better to go on to Korcula, where she would be hidden among other tourists and could escape in another direction if necessary.

Not that it would be. The look on Kinnan's face had convinced her that he would never pursue her again.

It was late afternoon before Alix finally disembarked from the ferry launch which had brought her from Orebic to Korcula. Wearily, she lifted her rucksack for the last time—she hoped—and looked around her.

It was, she had to admit, a pretty place. On the short trip across the strait she had been able to see the old walled city, not unlike that of Dubrovnik, but smaller. The same round towers dipped their feet in the sea, the same stretches of wall were once patrolled by guards and lookouts. There was a harbour, with small boats tossing on the unsettled waves, and a quay where the larger coastal ferries docked. The Orebic ferry went to the other side of the town, which was built on a peninsula, and moored alongside a quay which was lined with palm trees hung with golden flowers. Alix's heart lifted a little and she looked around with the first touch of pleasure she had felt that day.

Aware of hunger and thirst after the long drive, she walked along the quay and into the town. There were several small restaurants and cafés, and she went into one and ordered coffee. She would have a meal later, but she couldn't resist a cream cake to go with her coffee. Comfort-eating, she thought wryly; but it would take more than a cream cake to console her for her loss.

And then without warning all the pain welled up inside her. She had known it was coming, known that the merciful numbness couldn't last. But she hadn't realised it was going to be quite so bad, and she sat staring blindly out of the window at the cobbled street, almost afraid to move, letting it wash over her like a cruel wave, a wave that would wrench her away from dry land and suck her under, holding her there, battering her helpless body against the rocks until there was no more life left in her.

Was it going to be like this for the rest of her life? she

wondered, feeling the tearing sensation in her breast that taught her what was meant by a broken heart. Was she never going to be free? Oh, Kinnan, she mourned, why did you do it? Why did you ever let me love you?

It seemed a long time before she was able to get up and leave the café. She moved stiffly, still beset by the pain that she felt would never leave her now, paid her bill and walked out through the town. There was a tourist office opposite the café and she went across and obtained maps and books. There seemed to be plenty to see—villages like Vela Luka and Rasisce; the old town itself, with its museums and the house where Korculans claimed that the famous Venetian explorer Marco Polo had been born; the Moreska dance, performed traditionally in July but for tourists every Thursday evening; and there were plenty of beaches if she just wanted to swim and sunbathe.

The perfect holiday island, in fact, she thought ruefully. If only she were still in holiday mood!

Then she shook herself mentally, telling herself not to be so childish—so soft-centred, Bernie would have called it. She had escaped, hadn't she? She ought to be *thanking* Vita—hadn't the journalist told her she was doing her a favour? Look at it that way, she admonished herself. You've had a lucky escape. You could have found out after you'd been married—and what then? Could you have gone on living with him, knowing just how mercenary he was? Could you have borne his children?

Take yourself in hand, this sensible inner voice went on. Forget him—oh, maybe you can't straightaway, not after all that happened. But put him out of your mind. Keep him there. It's the only way.

And make the most of the rest of your holiday, it added. You may never get the chance to come here again. Don't waste this one.

Alix shrugged herself into her rucksack straps. The

little voice was right. Pity it hadn't been around when all this started. But it wasn't too late to start being sensible—and the first thing was to find somewhere to stay. . . .

An hour later, her luggage unpacked in a small, clean room that looked right down on the old town and the sea, Alix set out to explore. She had changed into clean jeans and a blue shirt that set off her dark gold hair, and she was carrying her camera—what luck that she hadn't lost that with her original luggage. She was, in fact, the typical tourist. And that was the way she intended to stay.

And it was the way she stayed for the next two or three days. She wore herself out, walking Korcula until she knew every nook and cranny; studying the museum exhibits, learning the history of the island; climbing the hills outside the town to look down on the terraced vineyards, many of them neglected now, and the walled olive groves. There were fig trees too, and a variety of other plants which testified to the fertility of the island and added to its beauty.

As well as walking, Alix took local buses to other parts of the island. She went to Vela Luka, at the far end, and admired the mosaic on the harbour, erected to commemorate a gathering of artists. Korcula was proud of its artistic tradition, she discovered, and traces of it could be discovered all over the island, mainly in its masonry and sculpture. She went to other villages too—Rasisce, where huge wine-barrels were being washed out at the waterside, and to Blato, the largest of the inland villages.

And all the time she was keeping a firm control on her longing for Kinnan. Whatever he had done, she found, it could not curb that yearning to be with him again. She still woke in the night, dreaming that his arms were about her, knowing fresh pain as she slowly realised that she was alone. She felt again the salty

kisses they had shared in the water; relived those
magical moments when they had made love in the
motor-boat under the blazing sky.

Rapture of the Deep, he'd called it. A diving term for
a condition that caused you to lose all your judgment,
take unnecessary risks and perhaps expose yourself to
deadly peril.

It was a good name for what had happened to her.
But she had escaped from the depths that caused the
condition now. She was back in shallower waters,
swimming free. And she would never get out of her
depth again.

By the end of the third day, Alix considered that she
had herself well in hand. She would be able to go back
to England completely in command of herself again,
able to tell her parents and Bernie what a wonderful
time she had had. Kinnan Macrae would be in the past,
where he belonged.

She was thinking this when she climbed to the tower
that stood on the hill immediately above the town.
From here, she expected to get a good view of much of
the island. And as she reached the top, walked round
the tower and faced down the hill to the tumbled roofs,
the dancing waters of the strait and the rugged line of
the mountains on the mainland, she smiled with
pleasure.

The scene was completed by a large yacht which was
making its way into the harbour. Long and graceful, it
was under full sail like a huge bird coming in to roost.
An unusual rig, she noted mechanically, remembering
those days when she had sailed with her uncle in the
Solent and learned to recognise many different yachts: a
Yankee jib, boomed stay-sail and mizzen. Just as
Kinnan had told her *Manta* was rigged.

A cold finger moved down her spine. No, it
couldn't be. How could he be here? How could he
know? But perhaps he didn't need to know. Perhaps

he was just searching ... determined to find her
again. . . .

Her blood thundering in her ears, Alix went down the
hill as if drawn by a magnet. She would be wise to keep
right away, that sensible inner voice warned her. Wise
to go nowhere near the harbour; wise to take a ferry
tomorrow to Split, Hvar, anywhere.

But the inner voice went unheeded. She wasn't going
to *see* Kinnan, after all—or at least, she wasn't going to
let him see her. But she had to know. If nothing else,
she just had to know.

CHAPTER TEN

THE ketch had gone up the creek, past Korcula town, when Alix emerged between the houses. There was no sign of it in the harbour and for a few minutes she stood irresolute. She knew that it was possible to walk right round the creek where the ketch was presumably anchoring; a narrow road led along the water's edge to a hotel and holiday complex. There would be little chance of hiding herself along the shore—if the ketch were *Manta*, Kinnan would only have to glance across the water to see her.

Perhaps she would be able to look down from the trees, where the road was higher and more hidden from the water. There were several houses along there, each with its own short stretch of waterfront. She would be less conspicuous there and she ought to be able to find out what she wanted to know. After that. . . .

After that, common sense told her, she would make tracks out of Korcula as fast as possible. Although, if indeed it were Kinnan and he were searching for her, it would surely take him some time to discover that she wasn't in Korcula. And he couldn't hunt her all the way up the Dalmatian coast and into Slovenia. She only had to stay one step ahead.

In which case, why shouldn't she stay and see the Moreska dance tomorrow evening?

It was crazy. She knew it was crazy. But she'd been looking forward to seeing the dance, which was only performed on this island. She'd bought her ticket. Why—why should she let this man spoil everything for her? Why *shouldn't* she stay, when she'd just begun to enjoy herself? Surely she could keep out of is way for a day? The island was large enough, for goodness' sake.

She passed the little *slasticarna* where she had often enjoyed a cake or ice from the array in the window, and walked along the narrow road. There were two more hotels here and she passed them, then came to the wooded stretch. Here were the houses, set below the level of the road; and it was only a few yards further before she could look cautiously down into the creek.

The ketch had anchored and the sails were already furled. A man Alix didn't know—a Yugoslav, she guessed—was busy on deck. She stared down, an odd feeling of disappointment tugging at her heart. *Wasn't* it *Manta*, then? But it looked so like her—the unusual rigging, the deckhouse, the shining white of the hull—could there be another ketch so exactly like the one where she had spent the past week?

And then another man came out on to the deck. He was tall, slim and muscular. A wave of coppery hair flowed back from his forehead and when he lifted his head and glanced up into the trees, Alix shrank back, suddenly afraid that those piercing grey eyes could see even through the sheltering branches, would find her wherever she tried to hide.

Kinnan Macrae had arrived on Korcula. But where were the others? Where was Jon—where was Vita? And just what was he really doing here?

Alix turned and made her way thoughtfully back to the town. What had happened? What had brought Kinnan to Korcula? Were Jon and Vita on board, still below deck? It didn't seem likely. Arrival at a new place must surely be an exciting moment for even the most blasé.

None of it matters to you, her inner voice scolded. Forget it—forget them, leave the island now—or tomorrow morning at the latest. Keep Kinnan Macrae out of your life.

But she knew she wouldn't do that. She had already
half-promised herself that she would stay one more
day—to see the Moreska. All she had to do was stay on
the alert and make sure that neither Kinnan, nor Jon or
Vita if they were with him, caught sight of her. That
wouldn't be hard—would it?

But it wasn't so easy, after all, to keep out of
Kinnan's way. In her heart, Alix knew that her best
course would be to take a bus to some inland village
where Kinnan would be unlikely to go. She could spend
the day there safely, come back to see the Moreska in
the evening, and leave Korcula by the first boat next
day. It was as simple as that.

Only it wasn't. Her thoughts were still in turmoil, her
feelings swerving violently from yearning to revulsion.
At one moment, she was recalling the magic of the
lovemaking they had shared, the rapture of knowing
that this was for life, that Kinnan loved her as much as
she loved him, that they would soon be married and
never parted again. Her dreams of diving with him in
the clear waters of the Caribbean or the Pacific invaded
her mind like a recurrent dream. A fairy-tale life, that
was what she had envisaged, and it was only with a
pain that wrenched at her heart that she could begin to
let her fantasy go.

And in the midst of her pain and longing, she would
remember Vita's words. Seeing the spite and malice
deforming the beautiful face, she could still not close
her ears to the words that still hissed in her brain.
Alison—the woman who had killed herself for
Kinnan—the woman who had left him all her money—
the woman who had made it possible for him to become
the success he was today, live the life he lived although
she could never share it. How could Alix give way to
her longings when the shadow of Alison must for ever
stand between them?

She still longed to be able to face Kinnan with her

doubts. The faint hope that he might be able to clear
them with a different truth still threaded through her
mind. But Vita had, very cleverly, made that
impossible, with a threat Alix dared not challenge.

No, the magical life she had visualised for herself
with Kinnan must remain for ever out of reach. But for
this one, last day, surely she could take what
consolation she could from his mere physical presence—
even if he remained unaware of her own. And so, taking
one last desperate risk, Alix did not take a bus to some
remote inland village; instead, she went down to the
creek early and watched from among the trees. When
Kinnan lowered the dinghy into the water and rowed
ashore with his Yugoslav companion, she kept watch
from a discreet distance on the quay where he moored
his boat and went ashore. And all that day, trembling in
case he should turn and see her, she followed him round
the narrow streets and alleyways of the old town,
watched as he played with the army of stray cats that
haunted the walls and the ruins, merged into crowds of
other tourists as he went in and out of museums and
climbed the staircase that was all that was left of Marco
Polo's supposed birthplace.

He didn't seem to be looking for her at all, she
thought as Kinnan finally returned to *Manta* at the end
of the afternoon. It was just a pleasure trip for him.
And she walked slowly back to her own room, feeling
oddly deflated. If she had not already bought her ticket
for the Moreska, she thought, she would probably have
left the island tonight. At all events, she would
definitely be on the ferry tomorrow morning.

Almost without thinking, she put on her Yugoslavian
blouse and skirt to go to the Moreska that evening.
Brushing her hair in the mirror, she stared into huge
green-and-gold eyes and asked herself what she had
been expecting. Had she been hoping that Kinnan

would see her? Hoping that, without her having to risk
Vita's wrath, they would actually meet again? Was that
why she'd followed him? Or had she really been making
absolutely sure that he wouldn't come upon her
unexpectedly, forcing her to face facts so unpalatable
that she had been trying to push them out of her mind,
unwilling to examine just what they meant. Neither
possibility was a comfortable one. She let the brush
drop to her side. Why was she letting Kinnan Macrae
upset her still, when it was all over? Why couldn't she
just shrug her shoulders and move on?

Abruptly, she turned away and pulled a light
cardigan round her shoulders before leaving the house.
For tonight, she would forget him and enjoy herself.
She'd been looking forward to this traditional and
picturesque dance, and she meant to enjoy it. At least it
wasn't the kind of thing Kinnan himself was likely to
attend!

But in that she was wrong. And she hadn't been
sitting in the large modern hall for ten minutes,
watching the throngs of people coming in, when a
movement at the end of her row made her look up
sharply, and her heart kicked as she found herself
looking up into eyes the colour of silver that seemed to
see right through into her brain, topped by the most
mobile and expressive pair of eyebrows she had ever
seen and a wave of thick, coppery hair. . . .

Alix could not speak. She watched helplessly as
Kinnan bent over to the man at her side. She listened
dumbly as she heard the man answer in German, saw
him smile at something Kinnan said and, to her
embarrassment, found the smile directed at herself
before the man got obligingly to his feet. Kinnan stood
back to let him pass, then took the vacant seat, while
the German made his way to another in the row behind.

'Well,' he said, a grim note in his voice, 'so we meet
again.'

Alix found her voice. 'What—what did you say to him?'

'I told him the truth, of course. That you are my fiancée, that we'd got separated after a misunderstanding, and that I'd be very grateful if I could sit beside you to share our pleasure in the performance. It's very colourful, I understand, and very romantic. It wouldn't be at all the same if I were not holding your hand.'

'Holding my—Kinnan, I am *not* going to sit here holding your hand!' Alix hissed. 'I don't know how you can—after all that's——'

'After all that's happened between us, were you going to say?' he enquired. 'After all that's happened between us, Alix, I should hope I might be allowed to hold more than your hand! Indeed, you didn't make much protest the other day, whatever I——'

'*Kinnan!*' Alix glanced round wildly, her cheeks burning. 'People will hear——'

'Don't tempt me to say things, then,' he returned, a glint in his eye that told her he meant what he said. 'I warn you, Alix, I've taken just about all I'm prepared to take. I mean to get this mess cleared up once and for all, and if I cause you a little embarrassment in the process that's just too bad. But it's up to you. If you just sit here quietly with me, holding my hand as a fiancée should, even throwing me the odd companionable word now and again—well, I won't need to embarrass you at all. And afterwards——'

'Yes?' she breathed, acutely conscious of his fingers entwined with hers.

'Afterwards we'll have a little talk,' he went on imperturbably. 'Where no one will see us, so that you can't be embarrassed. Where we'll be entirely alone, my dear Alix.'

Alix closed her eyes as a warm flush spread over her body. He could only mean *Manta*. He meant to take her aboard *Manta*—and once they were there, alone, what chance would she have? He had already proved that she couldn't withstand the attraction that still existed between them; that his assault on her senses could only be—from his point of view—successful. But from hers? Wouldn't it simply increase her confusion, her agony?

'Please, Kinnan,' she whispered as more and more people arrived in the auditorium, encircling the space cleared below the stage for the dancers, 'please don't. What use is it? I've tried—we've both tried—but it won't work, it can't. There's too much against us. Wouldn't it be far better if we could forget each other— forget we ever met?'

'And do you really think that's possible?' he grated, his fingers tightening painfully around hers. 'Do you think I haven't *tried*? Alix, you know you're talking nonsense. We're in each other's blood, don't you know that? Why else would I have come all this way to find you? Why else was I prepared to chuck everything, search until I had you beside me again? Any other girl, I'd have seen her on her way with my best wishes and hearty thanks for a lucky escape, but you—you're something else. I can't let you go like that!'

Alix looked at him with huge, tormented eyes. How was she to cope with this terrible yearning—the yearning that Kinnan had for her, the yearning she had for him? She wanted to give in, to relax in the love that he was offering—but what about Alison? What about Vita? Could it really last—or would it simply lead to more heartbreak?

She opened her mouth to speak again, but a sudden hush descended on the crowded hall. People were filing on to the stage; a woman was approaching a microphone. The performance was about to begin.

For the next two hours there was little chance of conversation. The Moreska itself was preceded by other traditional dances, performed mostly by teenage boys and girls, attractive dances which told a story, easily followed but in any case explained first in several languages by the woman at the microphone. The costumes were bright and colourful, and the skips and leaps produced a kaleidoscope of colour that at any other time Alix would have revelled in. But tonight her attention was taken up by the man at her side; all her emotions concentrated on the strong hand that held hers close, its warmth flowing through her fingers and into her blood; the arm that pressed against hers, reminding her of the times when it had encircled her body; the profile that, turned slightly away from her, appeared to be considering nothing but the dancers. But it was an illusion, Alix knew. One move from her and the whole of that formidable strength of mind and body would be turned upon her, and there would be no escape.

All around them people were taking photographs, their attention absorbed by the dancers. If only she could be enjoying it too! And then the highlight of the evening arrived and the Moreska dancers themselves entered the arena.

If the costumes of the earlier dances had been colourful, these were magnificent. Two opposing armies, one in red, the other in black. Their leaders, glorious in scarlet and gold, black and silver; and the princess that both wanted for a bride, young and pure in silks and chiffons.

The story was easy to follow, although the verses were incomprehensible to Alix. But it was plain that the black prince wanted the girl for his bride and was prepared to abduct her to get his way. While the red prince was the one she truly loved, and who loved her enough to do battle to win her back.

Then the movements of the sword dance began, seven in all. A virile and violent swooping of the armies upon each other, accompanied by the swinging and the

clashing of the swords. The music was martial and
exciting, the battles realistic enough to have people on
the edge of their seats. Black and red swirled around the
floor, crossing swords, thrusting, flailing, lunging. Now
and then a soldier would fall to the floor, sometimes to
rise, sometimes to remain there, apparently helpless.
Until in the end all the black soldiers lay dead in the
centre of the arena, two young boys waved huge
banners over the pile of fallen bodies, and the red
prince claimed the princess for his own.

Alix relaxed—and found that she had been holding
Kinnan's hand in both her own. She looked down,
startled, at the strong brown fingers that lay in her lap,
the powerful wrist. A deep blush spread over her cheeks
as she hastily returned it and looked up at his face.

'Enjoy it?' he murmured ambiguously, and she bit her
lip.

'The dancing was very good.'

'Excellent,' he agreed gravely. 'And now, I think, for
the second part of our night's entertainment.'

'I'm not——' Alix began, but she was silenced by the
voice of the leading Moreska dancer beginning a
speech. When that was over, there was the slow process
of getting out; a moment when she might have escaped
had it not been for Kinnan's fingers like steel around
her arm. And when, at last, they were outside in the
warm night air, Alix found that her protest had died.
Instead she found herself under a strange fatalistic spell.
The whole thing seemed inevitable. There was nothing
she could do about it, no way she could stand out
against Kinnan's determination. She might as well go
with him, get it over. Only then, perhaps, would she be
able to get on with her own life.

She seemed to retreat from herself, almost in a dream
as he led her across to the quay and handed her down
into the dinghy. And it was in the same dream that she
sat in the stern, gazing absently at the lights of the town

and the hotels as Kinnan, with swift, easy strokes, rowed them across the quiet starlit bay and into the creek where *Manta* swung gently at anchor like some huge, roosting bird and waited for the last act of the drama to be played out.

Alix was still in her fatalistic trance as the dinghy reached *Manta*. She waited submissively while Kinnan fastened the painter and climbed nimbly aboard. She gave him her hand when he leaned down, and followed him through the deckhouse and into the saloon. Almost with an air of detachment she sat down on one of the berths and waited while Kinnan turned up the lamp.

It was odd to be back. She seemed to have been away for so long—a lifetime, almost. She looked round with the kind of polite interest she might have shown on having tea with someone in a new house.

'Where are Jon,' she asked, 'and—and——' But she wasn't so detached after all; the other girl's name stuck in her throat.

'Jon's still in Dubrovnik,' Kinnan replied deliberately, 'and I haven't the least idea where Vita is. Not where I told her to go, I don't suppose, though I don't doubt she'll end up there some day if she doesn't mend her pretty little ways.'

Alix tried to sort that out in her mind but failed. She felt inexpressibly weary. So they were alone—except for——

Kinnan interpreted her look and added: 'And Josef's spending the night with relatives. There's no one else aboard.'

Alix nodded. It was all quite clear, then. Clearly there was no escape from the inevitable. Better get it over as quickly as possible, then Kinnan would let her go. She thought of Mrs Gladstone's injunction to lie back and think of England, and found herself smiling a little. It could almost apply to her—if she kept her mind on her return to England, to normal life, she might just be able to get through the ordeal without giving herself away.

Kinnan was watching her narrowly. 'What's the joke?'

Alix shrugged. 'I was just thinking—what are you waiting for? I'm here. No one will hear me if I scream, so I might as well not bother. Why don't you get on with it? Have your wicked way with me. That's what you brought me here for, isn't it?'

His face darkened. 'And you'd let me?'

'Wouldn't have much choice, would I?' She taunted him with her eyes. 'You said once it was the only way to get me out of your system. Well, if that's really true . . .!'

Kinnan made an explosive sound. As Alix reached towards him, he wrenched himself away, and she drew back as if she'd been stung. 'What's the matter?' she demanded, her heart jerking. 'Don't you want me?'

'Want you? Of course I bloody want you!' he snarled. 'But not like that. God, Alix, can't you see——' He ran anguished fingers through his hair and flung himself onto the opposite berth. 'Look, this is our last chance. Don't let's wreck it now, for God's sake. I'm begging you, Alix—come out of that glass cage you've built round yourself and be real again. Like you were when we first met—like you were in the boat the other day.'

'Real?' she repeated stupidly. 'Aren't I real?'

'No, you're not. You're like a doll. You're like a person frozen in a glacier—perfect to look at, but ice inside. Alix, thaw out, let me get at you, be *yourself* again. It's our only hope!'

Alix stared at him, then looked down at the table. She explored her feelings gently. He was right—she was frozen. There was nothing there. No emotion, no sensation. No pain—and no ecstasy. Would it ever return? Would she ever be able to feel again?

Suddenly terrified, she leapt to her feet and hurled

herself round the table into his arms. Sobbing with panic, she clutched at him, felt his arms encircle her, pulled frantically to get him closer. She sought his lips with hers and pressed her face into the pulsing throat.

'Thaw me, Kinnan,' she begged. 'You're right—everything's gone. I can't—I can't get it back, I can't be myself. I don't know what's happened to me. Make it right again, Kinnan, *please!*'

She felt the salt tears run down her cheeks and into her mouth; felt Kinnan lick them away before his own lips took hers with a tenderness that shook her to the bone. His arms were warm and comforting, without passion, his body firm and reassuring against hers. As she lay against him, she felt herself relax, she felt the life seep back into her as warmth seeps into chilly limbs after a cold swim. She breathed more evenly, nestled closer and laid her cheek on his chest to feel the strong heartbeat within. Perhaps they could stay like this for ever, she thought; perhaps no painful explanations were necessary after all.

But Kinnan evidently thought differently. Lifting her gently away from him, he said: 'It can't be made right just like that, though. You know that, don't you? We have to talk—sort out what's gone wrong between us, and see if we can make anything out of what's left.'

'Talking just makes things worse,' Alix whispered, and he shook his head.

'Only when we don't listen as well. Alix, we have to be absolutely honest with each other—and with ourselves. Nothing less will do.'

There was a silence. Alix was calmer now, but her feelings were still confused. She sat up and shook back her long brown hair, looking doubtfully at Kinnan. What did he want her to say? And couldn't this all be just a way of pulling the wool over her eyes, presenting the facts in his own favour?

'First of all,' he said, and his tone was grim again,

'just why did you run off like that, without any explanation?'

'Didn't Vita tell you? I'm sure she must have had some reason ready for you.' Alix was still cautious, still on the defensive. Her feelings might have thawed, be no longer so dreadfully frozen and numbed, but she was no surer of Kinnan than she had been before.

'We'll leave Vita out of this!' he grated, and she bit her lip. How *could* they leave Vita out of it, when she had engineered the whole thing?

'There you go again,' she said, her voice trembling. 'You say we have to be honest, we have to listen, and then you refuse to listen to the first thing I say. It's one law for you and another for me, isn't it?'

Kinnan sighed and ran a hand through his thick hair. 'All right, Alix, you're right. It's just that—well, if you must know, I've suffered one hell of a lot from Vita Purvis and I'm just about ready to pretend she never existed. I've thrown her off *Manta*, if you must know— oh, not literally, don't worry!—and told her to go to hell. Maybe she could write a feature about it!'

'You—you've done what?'

'I told you. Vita Purvis no longer comes anywhere near me.'

'But—but what about her father? The TV company? And her column—she could damage your whole career. I thought that was why——'

'You thought what?' He pounced like a hawk, his eyes sharpening. 'Come on, Alix—now that we're talking at last, tell me just what did you think?'

'I—I thought that was why you pretended to be engaged to me,' she muttered. 'Not because you were worried about *my* reputation—but for your own sake.' She stopped, but Kinnan motioned her to go on and she knew she would have to do so. 'Because you wanted to go into partnership with Vita's father, and while he would tolerate an engagement, even if it was broken at a later date, he wouldn't tolerate an affair. Well, it seemed quite likely,' she added defensively, seeing his expression grow grimmer. 'Max Purvis is well known for his religious beliefs, and his moral ones.'

'And what else did you think?' Kinnan pressed, his face like granite.

'That—that you'd be marrying Vita. She *told* me you would be.'

'For crying out loud,' he exclaimed, 'you didn't have to *believe* her, did you? Couldn't you see what type she was—is? Oh well, maybe I shouldn't blame you—she took me in once. And you're such an innocent—you're barely out of the egg. I suppose that's why I get this feeling I have to protect you, look after you——'

'Well, you needn't,' Alix flashed. 'I can look after myself! All right, so I was in a spot when we first met, and yes, you did help me—but I don't make a habit of getting into trouble and I don't need a man to take care of me and tell me not to bother my pretty little head! If that's the kind of relationship you have in mind, you can forget it!'

'It's not,' Kinnan retorted. 'I may feel I've got to be kind to dumb animals, but that doesn't mean I want to live with them. Whereas——' his voice grew ragged '—I *do* want to live with you, Alix, God help me. Look, let me tell you a few home truths about Vita. She and her father haven't spoken for years. He is, as you say, a moralist—he can't stand the way she lives and the way she earns some of her money, by repeating gossip about other people. He cut her off a long time ago—and Vita's been trying to get back in favour ever since. He's a rich man, you see. That's why she's so interested in me—because as his partner I'd stand to share in his success, as well as in my own. And as my wife, Vita would be back in favour. That was her theory, anyway.'

'I see.' Alix was silent, assimilating what Kinnan had told her. But it didn't really help—only explained a little more fully why the journalist had been so keen to get rid of her. The main stumbling-blocks still remained.

Kinnan was watching her narrowly. 'And just what other pretty little stories did Vita tell you?' he asked at length.

Alix hesitated. She was still reluctant to tell him; but he was determined to get it all out of her.

'You mentioned Alison,' he said at last, his voice hard. 'Would you mind telling me how Alison comes into this, and how you know about her? Okay——' he lifted a hand '—I can guess *how*. Tell me *what* you know—or think you know.'

'Only the facts,' said Alix, hurt and indignation welling in her on the other woman's behalf. 'Only that you had an affair with her—lived with her—took money from her—and then left her. Left her so lonely and unhappy that she killed herself, because you'd left her nothing to live for.'

It was out at last, the sordid little tale that had been festering in her heart ever since Vita had first told her. She stared defiantly at Kinnan, knowing at last that whatever the physical attraction, whatever the bond between them, she could never truly love a man who could behave in such a way; never live with him.

Kinnan stared back at her. His face was drained of all colour, his eyes were as hard as glass. Alix moved instinctively back into a corner. This must be the end. It had to be the end.

'Vita told you that?' he rasped at last. 'And you—believed her?'

Alix spread her hands helplessly. 'What else could I do? Facts like that could be traced.'

'You never even thought to ask *me*—just in case there was another version?'

'Yes, I did, of course I did!' she cried. 'I wanted to ask you—but Vita wouldn't let me——'

'Wouldn't *let* you? What sort of excuse is that?'

'A true one!' Alix took a deep breath. 'She—she threatened to ruin everything for you—your career, your prospects, everything. And she could *do* it, Kinnan! She—told me she followed me to Lokrum. She was watching when I went swimming—when I met you.' Her voice faltered and she added on a breath of sound: 'She had her camera with her.'

'I see.' Kinnan's voice was dry. 'And she threatened to expose us both—and what better word could I use!— in her column. Is that it?'

Alix nodded dumbly and he sighed. 'That column of Vita's! It's bugged us all the way along the line, hasn't it? Well, now I know what her last threats to me meant—but I don't somehow think she'll be carrying them out, Alix. You can set your mind at rest there.' He smiled grimly. 'Like I said, I'm in closer touch with Vita's father than she's been for years. I happen to know that he's just completing negotiations to buy the newspaper Vita writes for—and that column will be one of the first things to go! Vita will never write gossip again, Alix; even Fleet Street is sick of her. She'll make out all right on features, which she does well, so you needn't lose any sleep—but threats of the kind she's been making are empty ones now.'

'Oh. But if that's the case, why were you so worried in the first place? You must have known then——'

He grinned. 'Things weren't settled, though pretty near it. But mostly, it seemed a good way of keeping you around. And I had my own very personal reasons for wanting to do that.'

Alix looked at him wide-eyed as he ran a finger down her cheek. 'And—Alison?' she murmured.

'Ah yes, Alison.' He removed his finger and turned a little away from her. 'If it was ever worth it I'd sue Vita for the lies she's told about me and Alison. Not for my sake—for Alison's. But it will do no good to her now, and nobody who's important to me believes that tale. With one notable exception,' he added, turning back and giving Alix a look that brought a flush to her cheeks. 'And that's not really your fault. I ought to have told you before, but we never really had much time, did we?' He slid his arm round her shoulders, drawing her close. 'But these are the facts. Alix. Make your own judgment.'

Alix waited, her heartbeat loud in her ears, while Kinnan gazed reflectively at the lamp. Outside the waves lapped softly against *Manta*'s hull; across the creek came the sounds of holidaymakers walking along the road at the water's edge. Through the saloon window she could see the lights of the town, while the great bulk of the mountains blacked out the starlit sky.

'Alison was always interested in me,' Kinnan said at last, his voice low. 'Not surprising—she was my mother's closest friend, from their schooldays. They always kept in touch, though Alison went abroad when she married. When her husband died suddenly she came back to England and settled in the next village. She had no children and she never married again; perhaps that's why she always took a special interest in me—I was just a year old when she arrived and she was as much a part of my life as my mother and father.' He paused, marshalling his thoughts. 'I suppose Vita told you she was rich? Of course, she would—well, it was quite true. And my parents were perpetually hard up—my father was one of those vague, trusting people with no head for business. He went in for several ventures and few of them worked. By the time he died there was no money at all, and my mother went a year later, worn out with the struggle. I was just seventeen and it seemed natural enough to make my base with Alison while I finished school. She insisted I go on to university, and I knew that she derived a great deal of pleasure from seeing me get on. So I did. I took a degree in marine biology and I

learned to dive. When I left university I started to sell
my skills. There's quite a market for divers, you know,
and the pay's high. I worked hard and I did well. I
wanted to be able to pay Alison back for all she'd done
for me—by showing her that her faith in me was
justified, and by earning enough money to be able to do
things for *her*—not that she needed them, but I knew
she'd understand and appreciate them. Weekends away,
holidays, that sort of thing. I was all she had, you see;
my company was the most valuable thing I could give
her.'

He stopped, and Alix watched his face. It was a very
different story from the one Vita had told. She
wondered if the journalist had known the truth; if she
hadn't, it would surely have been easy enough to
discover. A wave of disgust swept over her as she
thought how the older girl had twisted the facts to make
something evil and sordid out of an act of simple loving
kindness, just to serve her own ends.

'There was never any more than that between Alison
and me,' Kinnan went on, and she knew without doubt
that it was true. 'I had girl-friends, plenty of them. God
forgive me, Vita was one. She bewitched me, in those
early days. I can only plead that I was young and had
inherited my father's habit of trusting too readily.
Unlike him, I soon learned better!' His voice hardened,
and Alix wondered what else there was in the story of
Kinnan and Vita, but guessed that she might never
know—that this was something that would remain
firmly in the past. 'And then Alison became ill. I wasn't
home much at that time—I was diving in the North
Sea. There was big money there and I wanted to earn as
much as possible to finance a project of my own. I
never knew she was ill—not until it was too late.' He
got up suddenly, turning away from Alix; then he
whipped round looking down at her and she flinched at
the agony in his eyes. 'It hurts even now,' he muttered.

'That she didn't tell me—that I was out there working all hours, just for money, while she. . . .' He visibly took a grip on himself and said harshly: 'She had cancer. A particularly painful form, totally incurable. She knew exactly what was wrong and how it would go, and she decided not to wait. She went in her own way, in her own time and with dignity.'

'Kinnan!' Alix breathed, her eyes wide with shocked distress. 'Kinnan, how awful—for her and for you.' She reached out blindly and found his hand, and the fingers closed around hers.

'Yes, it was awful,' he answered simply. 'But it was the way she wanted. I only wished I could have shared it with her in some way—but there was no question of that. She would never have risked the consequences of my knowing what she intended. That was why she waited until I was away—why she never let me know she was ill.' His eyes looked into Alix's, haunted grey into compassionate topaz. 'What makes it all much, much worse is the story that Vita's cooked up. My God, if I'd known just what she'd told you—I doubt if I could have kept my hands off her!'

They were silent for a moment, then he sat down again and Alix moved close, wanting to show him that Vita didn't matter any more. But there was more on Kinnan's mind, and after a moment he said: 'I've no doubt she told you that Alison left me all her money.'

Alix nodded. 'She said that was how you got started—how you could afford to set up your film company, buy *Manta*——'

He nodded. 'I thought so. Hell, she may genuinely believe that, I don't know. I never did publicise what I did with Alison's money. But I didn't touch a penny of it. I didn't need to and I wanted to make my own way. I gave it all to a charity for cancer research and relief. It seemed the most fitting way.'

'And—*Manta*?' Alix ventured.

'I told you, I was earning good money. But I wasn't spending it. I was researching a wreck I'd come across on one of my dives. I had a suspicion it was one of those ships that were lost during the war, carrying gold bullion—and I was right. When I was ready, I financed and led a salvage operation. We brought up over thirty tons of bullion, and it made me a millionaire.' He paused. 'Enough to keep me in luxury for the rest of my life—or to set up my own unit making the films I'd always wanted to make. Enough to reunite me with my first love—marine biology. Though as you may have noticed, I do like my comforts as well!' He smiled at Alix as she glanced around the luxurious fitments of the saloon. 'But everything I've got, I've worked for. None of it came easily—diving in the North Sea is a far cry from swanning around in the Adriatic or the Caribbean, I can tell you!'

Alix's head whirled. She could never have suspected the truth behind the lies Vita had told her—it all sounded so far-fetched. Yet she knew that every word of it was true. She had misjudged Kinnan all along the line. She had jumped to conclusions based on his lifestyle, without even stopping to wonder if she might be wrong, and she'd been more ready to believe the fabrication than the truth.

'I'm sorry, Kinnan,' she whispered. 'I should have trusted you.'

'And I should have trusted you,' he returned quietly. 'I should have told you the whole story when you told me about your brother and I realised what a hang-up you had about money. But I put it off until later—and it was almost too late. In fact, I'd have told you even before then, but I was angry at the assumptions you made and I made up my mind that I'd make you sorry for having come to such conclusions without any basis. That was wrong of me.'

'I've been thinking about Stephen,' Alix confessed.

'Even while you've been talking ... it wasn't the
money, really, was it? None of it had to happen because
of the money. It was his—well, his weakness, I
suppose.'

Kinnan shrugged. 'You'll have to make up your own
mind about that, Alix. But we can all blame outside
influences, when in fact we ought to be taking
responsibility for our own actions.... And talking of
taking responsibility,' he added, his eyes gleaming as he
drew her closer, 'what are we going to do with you for
the rest of the night? Do you want me to row you back
to Korcula, to sleep chastely in your bed? Or do you
stay here? Because I warn you, if you do, I'll not be
responsible for my actions....'

His hand slid down over her breast and she quivered
at the warm touch of his fingers. With a sigh of pure
bliss, she allowed him to lay her back on the long seat,
stretching her body like a cat as his fingers explored it
with assurance. 'Well?' he murmured, his lips against
her throat.

'Don't worry, Kinnan,' she whispered, letting her
own hands slide under his shirt to move over his back,
feeling the rippling muscles under her palms. '*I'll* take
responsibility ... it's the least I can do. And besides——'
She shivered as he drew the blouse over her head,
exposing the full breasts before he buried his face in
them. 'Besides—if I go now, it may all turn out to have
been a dream—and I couldn't bear that.'

'This is no dream,' Kinnan muttered, sliding out of
his own shirt so that he could press his skin against
hers, making them both gasp at the almost electric
shock of it. 'This is real—absolutely real. Dream later,
Alix my love—but for the next hour or two you'd better
believe it—all of it!'

ROMANCE

Variety is the spice of romance

Each month, Mills & Boon publish new romances. New stories about people falling in love. A world of variety in romance – from the best writers in the romantic world. Choose from these titles in June.

JILTED Sally Wentworth
HIGHLAND GATHERING Elizabeth Graham
A SUDDEN ENGAGEMENT Penny Jordan
ALL THAT HEAVEN ALLOWS Anne Weale
CAGE OF SHADOWS Anne Mather
THE GUARDED HEART Robyn Donald
LION'S DOMAIN Rosemary Carter
FACE THE TIGER Jane Donnelly
THE TIDES OF SUMMER Sandra Field
NIGHT OF POSSESSION Lilian Peake
PRICE TO BE MET Jessica Steele
NO ROOM IN HIS LIFE Nicola West

On sale where you buy paperbacks. If you require further information or have any difficulty obtaining them, write to: Mills & Boon Reader Service, PO Box 236, Thornton Road, Croydon, Surrey CR9 3RU, England.

Mills & Boon
the rose of romance

How to join in a whole new world of romance

It's very easy to subscribe to the Mills & Boon Reader Service. As a regular reader, you can enjoy a whole range of special benefits. Bargain offers. Big cash savings. Your own free Reader Service newsletter, packed with knitting patterns, recipes, competitions, and exclusive book offers.

We send you the very latest titles each month, postage and packing free – no hidden extra charges. There's absolutely no commitment – you receive books for only as long as you want.

We'll send you details. Simply send the coupon – or drop us a line for details about the Mills & Boon Reader Service Subscription Scheme.
Post to: Mills & Boon Reader Service, P.O. Box 236, Thornton Road, Croydon, Surrey CR9 3RU, England.
*Please note: READERS IN SOUTH AFRICA please write to: Mills & Boon Reader Service of Southern Africa, Private Bag X3010, Randburg 2125, S. Africa.

Please send me details of the Mills & Boon Subscription Scheme.
NAME (Mrs/Miss) _____ EP3
ADDRESS _____
_____
COUNTY/COUNTRY_____ POST/ZIP CODE_____
BLOCK LETTERS, PLEASE

Mills & Boon
the rose of romance